Jones 1963

Devin Cabrera

Chapter One

Jones Jepsen jumped down a flight of stairs, misjudging his landing and tumbling to the floor. His books scattered all around him, and he scrambled to pick them up.

From down the hall, he could hear the sounds of the people chasing him.

"Hey loser, wait up! We just want to talk!" came the voice of Robby Fletcher. Robby was the town's golden boy. He was the captain of the football team, the mayor's son, and he came from the richest family in Briarwood. His father owned almost every building in town and his brick factory was responsible for selling the materials needed to build everything else. In other words, Robby was untouchable.

A series of laughs rang out down the hall, and Jones knew that they were kidding about the talking part. His bullies had never been much for talking unless it was to call him a pansy or a loser.

When they weren't talking, they were constantly shoving him into whatever they could make him fit into. Usually, it was a full garbage can at the cafeteria, someone's locker, or the school principal, after which he would be punished for attacking a member of the school faculty.

Jones picked up what books he could and immediately began to run, he could do without the notes he left behind.

At the end of the hall, Robby's face appeared, followed by Max, Kyle, and Carol.

Each of them belonged to some of the wealthier families in town, families that paid the salaries of a majority of the town's citizens.

That meant that if this group were ever to get caught doing something awful, they would get a slap on the wrist, or else the punisher would lose their jobs in short order.

Jones saw a trash can up ahead, and when he looked back he saw that the group was gaining on him. When he got to the can, he pushed it over in front of them, spilling trash and causing a loud commotion in the hall.

Several teachers opened their classroom doors to see what the noise was. Others yelled at him to stop messing around and get to class.

Not a single one stopped to help him.

He was on his own.

Jones tried to turn into an empty room, but he immediately felt a tug on his backpack as he was yanked backward.

Jones fell to the floor, barely able to hold onto his books. He looked up and saw the face of Kyle, one of his tormentors.

Kyle grabbed him by the back of the shirt and began to drag him down the hall like a tarp full of leaves.

Jones squirmed around, trying to get out of Kyle's grip, but resistance was futile. Even if he could get away, the rest of the group had just arrived and would be able to catch him.

His best chance now would be to stop resisting and hope that his punishment wouldn't be too bad. Maybe if he gave them what they wanted, they would go easier on him.

It was a stupid thought, one that hadn't worked with him in the past no matter how much he tried it.

These kids had a plan for him in mind, and they wouldn't stop until they got what they wanted.

Typical spoiled brats.

Jones couldn't see where they were going, but he could see the faces of his classmates that they passed, each of them turning to laugh at him as he was dragged away.

He heard a door open and then felt the change in the flooring under his back. His next hint was the smell.

They had pulled him into the bathroom.

Carol stood watch outside while the guys dragged Jones toward the stalls.

The boys banged on each stall, trying to find one that was unoccupied, but all of them were full.

"EVERYONE OUT, OR YOU WILL BE NEXT!" Kyle shouted.

The bathroom rang out with the sound of several toilets flushing at once, and one by one the stalls emptied. The fleeing boys didn't even bother to wash their hands, which Jones acknowledged was a weird thing to think about at this time.

Jones felt his body being dragged once more as Max kicked open a stall door and lifted the toilet seat.

"You're going in!" Kyle said, laughing with his buddies.

"No, no, NOOO!" Jones shouted as his legs were lifted over his head. He placed his hands on the edge of the bowl to prevent them from dunking his head inside, and he gagged at how wet his hands suddenly became.

Boys were disgusting, he thought to himself.

While Max and Robby were holding his legs, Kyle swept Jones's arms out from under him and he found himself plunging into the waters of the toilet below.

He screamed, but only bubbles came out.

Jones felt like a starfish or one of those other fish that cling to the fishbowl and clean the scum off of it with their mouths. He didn't want to think of what happened in that toilet on a daily basis, especially considering how recently he had seen someone leave the stall.

Through the water, he could hear the muffled sounds of the boys laughing at his expense.

Jones thought he could see dark stains on the porcelain, and he closed his eyes. Nothing good would come from having them open.

Suddenly, the boys dropped Jones to the floor, and he would soon find out why.

Loud shouting could be heard coming from the hall, and Jones felt a tug on the back of his shirt as he was lifted to his feet.

The boys all turned as the door to the bathroom slammed open.

There stood a red-faced Mr. Pickering, the school principal. The man was overweight, a fact that made him breathe heavily no matter how fast he walked places. He had hair only on the sides of his head, but the top was as smooth as an egg. It gleamed under the fluorescent lighting in the bathroom, and it was just as red as the rest of his face. He wore a sweater vest over a button-up shirt, even though it was the end of spring.

Mr. Pickering was known for his temper toward misbehaving kids, but also for his favoritism toward students whose parents paid his salary.

He stopped in his tracks, obviously not expecting so many people to be in the room with him, especially not the golden boys of Briarwood High.

Through the door, they could see Carol mouthing the words "I tried" as she backed away from the room.

"I'm getting reports of screaming and running in the halls, disrupting classes and the like. What is the meaning of all this?" Mr. Pickering said, gesturing to Jones's wet face and clothes.

Jones puffed out his cheeks, breathing heavily as he spit out the last of the toilet water in his mouth.

Mr. Pickering looked down on Jones with disgust. Not only because he was covered in toilet water, but because most of the people in Briarwood tended to look down on the members of his family.

Jones thought that for once, somebody was standing up for him, that for once, somebody was going to make the boys pay for their actions.

"Jepsen? Aren't you going to answer me?" Mr. Pickering asked.

"I- uh..." Before he could say anything else, he felt a hard pinch on his back and realized that Robby was holding him. He knew that if he said anything bad about them, they would punish him for it later.

"Jones isn't feeling very well right now, Mr. Pickering," Max said. "We saw him screaming and hollering down the hall, pushing people out of his way and making a mess, so we followed him, to get him to stop his foolish antics. We brought him into the bathroom and splashed some water on his face because we assumed he must have fallen asleep in class. We figured that he was one of those sleep-walking kids, and the only way to fix him would be to wake him up. Isn't that right, Jones?"

With that, Max turned to face Jones, and his expression told him to go along with it or he was dead.

"That isn't.." Jones felt another pinch in his back as Robby's grip got tighter.

"I mean, that's right Mr. Pickering. That's the god's honest truth right there." Jones said, staring down at the floor.

Mr. Pickering looked him up and down in disgust.

"Sleepwalking, eh? That's the excuse you're going with?" Mr. Pickering wiped the sweat from his brow. "Boys, get back to class this instant."

The boys all made their way to the door, but Mr. Pickering stopped Jones in his tracks.

"Not you, Mr. Jepsen," Mr. Pickering said.

From the hallway behind him, Jones could see the boys miming a knife across their throats at him.

Chapter Two

Mr. Pickering took a seat in his chair, leaning back as far as he could go, with the chair protesting loudly as he did so. He kicked his feet up on the desk and reached into his chest pocket, producing a crumpled pack of cigarettes and a lighter. He slapped the pack against his palm a few times before selecting one of the cancer sticks.

Mr. Pickering brought it to his mouth and inhaled deeply as he lit the thing. He closed the lighter with a flick of his wrist, tossing it into a drawer of his desk before taking another pull from his cigarette.

He leaned his head back and blew smoke into the air, the whole time staring at Jones.

Jones watched as the smoke curled in the air, illuminated by the sun's rays streaming in through the window.

Mr. Pickering just stared at Jones, contemplating his next move.

"What the hell am I gonna do about you?" he asked.

Jones had a few options of what he could say.

He could rat out the golden boys, at which point nothing would happen to them, and he would get his ass handed to him on a silver platter later. Or he could fess up and say that he suffered from sleepwalking, and be labeled as the crazy person in town for the rest of his days. Either way, this would make its way back to his father, and he would get an ass beating anyway.

He decided to go with the first option, hoping that that would lead to some kind of repercussions for the boys. Maybe they would get suspended, and he would get a few days without having to look over his shoulder everywhere he went.

"I don't actually suffer from sleepwalking," Jones said, staring down at his feet.

Mr. Pickering blew a puff of smoke into the air, watching as it curled and eddied away from him.

"Yeah, no shit," Mr. Pickering said.

Jones looked up, he wasn't expecting Mr. Pickering to say that.

"Those boys were giving you a swirlie in the bathroom, weren't they? Or at least that's what I hope you all were doing in there, otherwise, I'd have to send you over to the guidance office to talk to someone else about what happened," Mr. Pickering said.

"Yeah! Those boys have been picking on me for years, and nobody has ever done anything about it," Jones said.

"And nobody will ever do anything about it," Mr. Pickering said, stubbing out his cigarette and waving away the smoke.

"I don't understand," Jones said. "You just said that you knew that they were bullying me. You're not going to help me?"

"Listen, kid," Mr. Pickering began, getting up and walking over to the window, opening it and giving a place for the smoke to escape. "You have to pick your battles, and this is one that you are going to lose every time. You are at the bottom of the food chain, and those guys are at the top. The rabbit doesn't pick a fight with the lion, you understand what I'm saying, kid?"

"Not at all," Jones said dumbfoundedly.

"You come from poor stock, and those group of boys come from the richest families in town. Their families own everything, and their taxes and donations pay for half the stuff on this campus. When it comes between you and them, people are going to pick them every time. That's the way that life works, and you're going to have to learn that lesson real quick or you're not going to survive very long in the real world. Do I like their parents? Not very much. But do I kiss up to them every time they come around so that the school can continue to receive financial support from them? Absolutely. Because the world runs on money and the ones that have it control everything. The less you have, the less people care about you." Mr. Pickering turned away from the window, where he had been admiring one of the English Literature teachers for the last few minutes.

"So what you are saying is that you are not going to help me?" Jones asked.

"I'll tell you what," Mr. Pickering said. "I won't punish you for creating a disturbance in school today, and I won't be making a call to your father. Lord knows that man could whip the hide off a bull if he wanted to, and nobody deserves a punishment like that. But I do ask that you refrain from antagonizing those boys any further, as it will only lead to your downfall in the end. If you can't make it here, maybe follow in the footsteps of your brother and join the army. At least that way you could get away from these boys and make a name for yourself.

Chapter Three

"Jepsen comma Jones," an army recruiter shouted down the hall. Jones snapped to attention, realizing that his name had just been called.

He got up from the folding chair he was sitting in and rushed towards the recruiter. As he walked down the hall, he passed several young men around his age, all in button-up shirts and greased-back hair. The young men of Briarwood were all trying to look their best as they signed up for the army. They were all hopeful that they would be able to go overseas and fight for their country.

Jones arrived in front of the folding table that the recruiter was using as a makeshift desk.

The recruiter looked up from his folder to check out Jones's form, then looked back at his paperwork. "It says here that you passed your physical, have no allergies, twenty-twenty vision, and have all your shots. I am hereby approving you for enlistment." With that, the recruiter took a wooden stamp, pressed it on a fresh ink pad, and then brought it down on Jones's form, leaving a bright red "Approved" label right next to his picture. He handed the forms to Jones before saying "Go take these to the woman at the next table and they will assign you a draft date. Thank you for enlisting and may god have mercy on your soul. Your country thanks you. Next!"

Jones Jepsen walked out of the Elks lodge with a smile on his face. He had passed his physical and would be able to serve his country as his brother and father had.

He was a good-looking kid who had just turned 18. His brown eyes gleamed as he walked, his chin was sharp enough to cut glass and his long dark hair was gelled up and towards the back of his head. He knew that in the army he would have to shave his head, so he tried to enjoy the length of his hair while he still had the chance. Jones was tall and skinny, and some kids called him String Bean for it.

Jones picked up his pace, his excitement growing as he neared his destination.

Briarwood was a suburban town, each house going up around the same time and looking exactly the same as the house next to it. If you didn't know where you were going, you might think you were in a mirrored universe that never ends, as you continued to walk down a street where the houses repeat themselves.

Jones turned down Bleeker Street, spotting the house that he wanted. The number on the mailbox read 57, and as he walked through the gate of the white picket fence, Jones bent down and plucked a flower from the garden. It was a white daisy, with a solid yellow circle in the center. Its petals were perfect, undamaged by the sun and the insects. Jones took a whiff of the flower, rejoicing in the smell it provided.

This will do perfectly, Jones thought to himself.

He strolled up to the front door, knocked on it three times, and waited as he heard footsteps approaching. The handle turned, and the door whooshed open to reveal a gorgeous blonde girl.

Peggy Myers stood in the doorway, her hourglass figure accentuated by the floral dress which showed off her long legs. Her eyes lit up when they saw Jones and seemed to get even brighter when they saw the flower.

"For me?" she asked. She threw the back of her hand against her forehead, feigning like she was about to faint. "Wherever did you get such a beautiful flower?"

"I didn't have to go too far," Jones said. He stepped aside, revealing Peggy's garden behind him.

They both shared a laugh, and then Jones swept in, picking Peggy up and twirling her around before bringing her in for a kiss. As the sun shone down upon them, Peggy wrapped her arms around his neck, willing him closer with every second that passed by.

At this moment Jones felt like he had never been happier in his life.

After a few seconds, they heard a low grunt coming from nearby.

They pulled apart, and Jones noticed for the first time that Peggy's father was standing in the front door behind her.

Kenneth Meyers was a well-built and well-put-together man. What hair he had left on his head was slicked back and tidy. His shirt was tucked in and there was not a crease to be had on his pants. The man's shoes gleamed to the point where Jones could see his reflection, and it reminded him that he should keep his chin up when addressing his future father-in-law.

"Mr. Meyers," Jones said, releasing his hold on Peggy and reaching out to shake the man's hand. "Such a pleasure to see you again."

The man shook Jones's hand, although there was a look of disdain in his eyes. It was clear that he didn't approve of Jones dating his daughter.

"Well don't be a stranger, come on in," came a voice from behind him.

A hand shot out from Mr. Meyers's side and moved him out of the way as Mrs. Meyers ushered Jones inside.

Mrs. Meyers was a frail old woman. She was only in her late forties, but living in hard times tends to age a person much faster than they should. Her hair had gone prematurely gray and her forehead was creased with wrinkles. One feature that she had that Jones had never seen in his own parents was smile lines. This woman tended to smile like it was her job, as she tried to be as welcoming as can be to anyone she was around.

The Meyers family didn't have much, but Mrs. Meyers still made sure to make a basket of muffins to pass out at Church every Sunday. She made it her business to go around and make sure that everyone at the service had been fed.

It made sense therefore that the person who was so beautiful on the inside had created a daughter who was so beautiful on the outside.

"Come on in," Mrs. Meyers repeated, wiping her hands off on the apron drooped around her waist. She brought Jones in for a hug, not because they were that friendly but because she was like that with everybody. "Don't mind my wet hands, I was in the middle of washing the dishes."

Jones entered the Meyers residence, stepping into a small, cozy living room adorned with vintage furniture and framed family photographs. The room was illuminated by the soft glow of a table lamp, casting a warm ambiance. It was the same layout as Jones's own house, as they were the same model, but this house seemed a lot more inviting than his house ever felt.

Mrs. Meyers walked back into the kitchen to finish clearing up, leaving the couple alone with her father, who stood there awkwardly as a third wheel.

Jones smiled at Peggy, whose bright blue eyes beamed back up at him. He couldn't wait until he could spend the rest of his life with that girl, but first, he needed to save up for a ring, a feat that he hoped enlisting in the army would help him afford.

He squeezed Peggy tightly, which made Mr. Meyers let out another small grunt. Apparently, he didn't like the idea of public displays of affection between his daughter and a member of the opposite sex happening under his roof, especially not in front of him.

Jones and Peggy stepped away from each other but shared a smirk across the room.

"Jones, can I have a word with you for a moment?" Mr. Meyers asked. He looked at Peggy meaningfully, and she seemed to understand the look.

"Right, I'm gonna go see if mother needs any help in the kitchen," Peggy said.

Jones's heart skipped a beat, but he nodded and followed his girlfriend's father to a corner of the living room.

"Peggy means the world to me," Mr. Meyers said. "She's my only daughter."

She was also an only child, but Jones felt like this might not be the best time to bring this point up.

"I understand, Mr. Meyers. I care about her deeply, and I'll always treat her with respect and kindness," Jones said.

"Good. Just remember, I've seen a lot in my years. I know the temptations and distractions that come along with being young. My daughter deserves someone who will stand by her."

"I want to be that person, sir. I want to be there for Peggy, to support her dreams and ambitions."

Mr. Meyers sized Jones up with his eyes.

"I don't think it's a secret that I don't like you very much, and I wish that my daughter would date someone with a better standing in life. But as long as you make her happy, that is all I care about. As long as you can manage to maintain her happiness, you have my approval to date my daughter."

"I promise I won't let you down sir," Jones said. His face grew red at the mention of his social standing. His father had a bit of a reputation that preceded Jones everywhere he went. There was a certain stigma that came along with it, which meant that before he was able to form a new opinion of himself in the eyes of others, he was already being judged by the actions of his father.

Mr. Meyers nodded in approval, and he walked back to the kitchen and sent his daughter into the living room with Jones.

"Did my father give you the third degree?" Peggy asked.

"Just a little friendly conversation," Jones said. "Sit down, there's something I have to tell you."

Peggy placed the flower on the table and took a seat, her worry deepening.

"You're making me anxious, Jones. What's going on?" Peggy asked.

Jones took a deep breath, struggling to find the right words. He walked over to where Peggy sat, kneeling in front of her and taking her hands in his.

"Peggy, you know how much I love you right? We've been through so much together," Jones said.

"Of course, but why are you acting so serious?" Peggy asked.

"I enlisted, Peggy. I've joined the military and... I'm being deployed to Vietnam," Jones said.

Peggy released her hands from his, placing them over her mouth.

"V-Vietnam? Jones, you...you can't be serious," Peggy said.

"I didn't want to keep this from you, I wanted you to know the truth," Jones said.

Peggy's shock turned into a mix of sadness and anger, as tears began to well up in her eyes.

"You're leaving me? Going into a warzone? Jones, this is so dangerous!"

Jones wiped a tear from Peggy's cheek and held her hands tightly.

"I know Peggy. I know it's dangerous, and I'm scared too. But I couldn't just stand here and get berated by my father about how brave my brother was for going into the army. I couldn't stand back and watch as the other men of Briarwood enlisted and went out to fight for our freedoms. I didn't want to stay here and end up working for the brick factory like my father."

Peggy sniffled, her eyes locking onto Jones.

"And what am I supposed to do while you're away Jones? Wait and worry every day?"

Jones's expression was one of regret and determination. He hated making Peggy feel this way, but he knew it was something that he had to do.

"No, Peggy. I want you to live your life, and chase your dreams.

Promise me that you'll stay strong, that you'll keep hope alive. When I come back, we'll build a future together, just like we've always talked about."

Peggy's tears flowed freely now as she nodded, her grip on Jones's hands firm.

"I promise."

Jones pulled Peggy into a tight embrace, holding her close as they shared a bittersweet moment.

"Thank you, Peggy. Your love means the world to me," Jones whispered in her ear.

Chapter Four

Jones walked up the sidewalk outside his home. He fixed his tie, straightened his posture, and thought of how he was going to tell his family. He stopped in front of the door, taking a breath to calm himself.

He grasped the handle, but the door was locked.

His parents weren't home, they must have been shopping, Jones thought.

Nobody in town locked their doors, it was a safe place. Some would think that his parents were just being cautious, but Jones knew better. He knew that his father was doing it intentionally to lock him out. He didn't trust him. Ever since his brother died, his father looked at Jones like the piece of shit who should've died in that war. He looked at him as the one that he was stuck with.

Jones went and sat on the curb, waiting for his parents to get home.

A cold breeze drew in from the west, and leaves tumbled down the street in a spiral formation.

It carried with it the sound of little girls playing, and Jones looked up to see the Shafer twins playing Double Dutch down the road.

The Shafer twins were eleven years old and identical in every way. They had curly brown hair which bounced on their blue and white checkered dresses as they jumped rope.

"Ring around the rosie," the girls sang in unison as the jump rope smacked the pavement.

Jones thought about how he would tell his parents.

"Pockets full of posies."

He thought of the reaction they would have. Would it be joy? Stepping into the footsteps of his brother?

"Ashes, ashes."

Would they finally be proud of him?

"We all fall down!"

Bang!

A car backfired, and Jones looked up to see his father's old Buick rumbling down the street toward him.

The thing was covered in rust, and although Jones didn't notice it at the time, it caught the attention of the Shafer twins, who promptly ran away as the car approached. They knew what wrath his father brought, even at a young age, and they didn't want to get in the middle of it, to have the direction of his onslaught turned toward them.

From Jones's spot on the curb, he heard his father screaming at his mother. It was loud enough that he could hear it clearly through the car, which meant that the whole neighborhood knew exactly what they were arguing about.

Jones decided that the conversation about the army would be best to be had at a different time after his parents had cooled off a bit.

He waited until after his parents went into the house before entering himself, he didn't want to get in the middle of whatever today's argument was about.

Jones opened the door slowly, and he heard shouts coming from the living room. He quietly walked to his room, closing his door behind him.

Jones's room was just like any other boy's room on his street, or so he thought. He had never actually been invited over to any of the houses of the guys he went to school with.

His bed was just a cot on the floor. His family wasn't able to get him a proper bedframe or a box spring, as every dollar that they got went into providing a roof over their heads and food on the table.

At least, that's what his dad liked to say between sips of his latest beer and drags from the cigarette he was smoking at the time.

Jones liked to think that if his father would spend less money on products he used to try to forget his situation, then they could probably afford to be in a better one.

But if Jones were to bring up anything of the sort to his father, it would only result in his bare ass getting beat raw by his father's belt.

Jones found himself in that situation quite often, not so much for being a bad child but for the fact that his father was a raging drunk who liked to take out his frustrations on the people and things around him.

"Dinner is ready!" his mother called to him from the other room.

Jones got up from his bed, crossing to the other side of the room where a mirror stood against the wall above his dresser. He moved in real close to the mirror, checking his skin for acne and brushing a stray hair behind his ear.

He grabbed a toy plane on his dresser, feeling the individual rivets bolted into the steel hull. His fingers brushed against the paint job, the span of the wings, and finally, he flicked the propeller, watching as it spun to a stop.

The model plane was a gift from his brother on the last day he saw him. The day before he left for...

"Your mother said that dinner was ready!" His father screamed from the other room.

Jones squeezed the toy plane one last time.

"Wish me luck," he whispered to the plane before dropping it back onto the dresser.

Taking one last moment to straighten his tie in the mirror, Jones walked out of his bedroom.

He saw something flying through the air and ducked just in time, narrowly avoiding getting hit with a plate full of mashed potatoes. The plate smashed against the wall nearby, leaving the mashed potatoes to slide down the wall in off-white clumps.

"Relax, Dad, what are you doing? That looked like good mashed potatoes," Jones said. He stuck his finger into the mess dripping down the wall and then proceeded to stick it into his mouth. "Mm, dinner tastes wonderful Mom."

"Relax? You're gonna tell me to relax?" Jones's father said. He bent down and picked up an auburn-colored glass ashtray. He was about to throw it at Jones, when he looked down at the tray and thought better of it. Not because he didn't want to hit his son with an object that could give him a concussion or cut his eye out, but because he spent a lot of time with the ashtray and cherished its existence by his side.

Jones used the distraction to slip into the dining room.

As Jones entered the dining room, his father got up from the recliner in the corner of the living room, stumbling to his feet.

His father was already drunk and they hadn't even had dinner yet, which wasn't surprising as he tended to do this every day. The recliner was where his father spent the bulk of his time during the day. When he wasn't eating or relieving himself, he was in that chair, smoking and drinking until he couldn't remember his own name. The ceiling above his chair was stained a dark yellow from all the smoke, and it felt like his mother had a full-time job cleaning up all the bottles that lay around him on a daily basis. Nobody else would dare to sit in his chair, or risk getting a beating from him. He spent so much time there that when he got up, there was a permanent imprint of his ass on the seat.

The chair was facing the living room window, where he spent the day watching as new residents moved into the homes nearby, and he would complain about how the neighborhood was going to shit with all of these new people coming in. On days when people weren't moving in, he would watch the window, waiting for the mailman to come to deliver his next disability check.

Jones scowled at the man. There was nobody on earth that he hated more than his own father. He thought the man was a waste of human flesh, and his father no doubt thought the same about him.

Jones fixed his face as his father regained his composure. Anything that may not be considered an adoring look towards his father could end up in an ass-whooping for him. It all depended on how drunk he was and how long it had been since the last disability check had come in.

His mother was finishing up, carefully placing each dish on the table. She didn't want to place them too hard or the loud noise may set off her husband, who tended to be sensitive to such things after he had been drinking.

Jones noticed that the bowl of potatoes that had been thrown across the room earlier had been refilled, his mother must have worked double time to make a new batch to his father's liking this time.

Jones pulled the chair out for his mother to have a seat at the dining room table before taking a seat himself. He put his hands together trying to figure out the best way to tell his family that he had enlisted into the army.

His father took a seat at the head of the table, letting out a whoosh of air as if it was so exhausting moving from one chair to another.

Jones took a deep breath, steadying himself before saying "There's something I have to tell the both of you."

His father slammed the palm of his hand down on the table, making all of the dishes rattle as he did so.

"I just sat the fuck down. I'm not hearing anything from anybody until we say grace," his father said.

His mother reached out a hand to each of them. Jones took it, then reluctantly slid his hand towards his father, who grabbed it and gave it a rough squeeze like a man trying to impress another with a firm handshake.

Mrs. Jepsen cleared her throat and then began her prayer.

"Our Father, who art in Heaven, please look down upon us and give us thy blessing. Please bless Jones in all of his ventures..."

To this, his father harumphed loudly.

Jones didn't even bother to look up, he knew his father would be grimacing at the terms mentioned in this prayer.

"Oh heavenly father, please let Mr. Jepsen continue to receive the disability checks that allow us to keep a roof over our heads and food in our stomachs. Amen"

"Amen," the men said in unison.

Jones's father pressed his fingers to his lips, kissed them, and raised them toward the heavens.

"I've said it before and I'll say it again. The man upstairs is the reason that I'm still alive today. Without him, I probably would have stepped on that landmine and I wouldn't have been here today. Instead, poor James Stewart stepped on it and I only received partial shrapnel damage to my leg. It just wasn't my time, I guess." His father made the sign of the cross over his chest and then dug into his food.

Jones couldn't help but think of how the lord must have been punishing him by allowing his father to only be a witness to the blast and not bear the full force of it. The man had been grazed by a piece of shrapnel which barely scarred him, but he had claimed that he had an unseen pain and had been riding the disability checks ever since.

Jones waited until his father had filled himself up with some steak and mashed potatoes. He figured that the man would be in a better mood if his stomach was full.

He put his utensil down by the sides of his plate, wiped his mouth with the corner of his napkin, and then cleared his throat.

"There is something that I wanted to tell you both," Jones started.

"What now?" Jones's father said, slamming his fork down on the table. "Can't a man get a moment to enjoy his meal in peace before someone starts running their mouth at the table?"

"I'm not running my… never mind," Jones said, beginning to regret starting the conversation. Then he stopped, taking a deep breath. He had to get this out and now was about as good a time as any. "No, in fact, I have to say this. I went down to the town hall this morning, where they were doing sign-ups for the war. I walked inside and did my physical, and I was cleared to enlist… So, I did."

Jones stopped to take a breath. He realized that he hadn't taken a breath the entire time he was talking, as he was so eager to get the words out. Now that he said them, he was so glad that he did, as the weight that had just been lifted off his chest was…

"YOU DID WHAT?" his father screamed.

The man got up from the table so fast that his chair flung backward into the wall, creating gouge marks where the top of the chair hit it.

"I enlisted in the army?" Jones said, getting up from his chair and backing away slowly.

He had seen his father angry, and it never went well, but he had never seen him this angry before.

"Why the fuck would you do such a stupid thing?" his father said.

"I thought that you would be proud of me. You served in the army. Steven served in the army…"

"Don't you dare mention my boy's name. You haven't earned the right to say his name in front of me," his father screamed, specks of spittle laced with potatoes spewing from his mouth.

"I thought that I could serve and do my part, just like you guys did," Jones tried to get out, as his father was currently rushing around the table towards him.

"I almost lost a leg in the war. Your brother lost his life protecting our country. And you want to mock his memory by going out and making fun of what he did? As if you could do what he did. You're pathetic, and you would never be the man that he was."

"I wasn't making fun of him, I wanted to go out to war and be a hero like him," Jones said, taking a few steps around the dining room, putting the table in between himself and his father, whose face seemed like it was about to burst.

The veins in his head looked like they were about to pop, and the saliva pooled up around the edges of his lips as he screamed.

"So now you want to go out and play hero, is that it? You want to go out and get yourself killed like your brother, and leave your poor mother here childless, with two dead sons?" His father made a break to the left, but Jones matched it, going the other way and missing him once more.

"I wasn't thinking that I was going to leave mom childless," Jones began.

"Of course not, of course you weren't thinking. When have you ever had a clear thought go through that thick, stupid skull of yours? I ought to kill you right now, to save us all the trouble. No need to have our country dish out my hard-earned tax dollars to send you over there to kill yourself, that money should go to someone who would make a difference, to someone who's not going to fuck around over there."

He made another pass to the left, faking Jones out and then going in the opposite direction. This time, he was able to get a hold of Jones, grabbing him by the shirt collar and yanking him down to his level, ripping the shirt in the process. Then he wrapped his thick, muscled forearms around Jones's throat and began to squeeze.

"Dad, I can't...I can't breathe," Jones tried to choke out. He looked towards his mother, who currently sat at the table with her arms crossed. A lit cigarette adorned her lips, and a tear slowly trickled down her face. He didn't know if the tear was for him leaving or for the way her husband was treating her son. Either way, she knew better than to get in between them. In the past, she had come away with one too many fat lips and black eyes, and she wasn't going to do that tonight.

"Mom...help," Jones pleaded, his eyes bulging out of their sockets as he tried to pry his father's arms from his throat. His attempts were useless, as his scrawny arms had nothing on the sheer girth that the man had taken on whilst drinking in his chair.

His mother just took another pull from her cigarette, then ashed it out on the tray in front of her.

He could see in her eyes now how she really felt. She felt like another of her boys was going out and trying to leave her. She felt that Jones was selfish, trying to go out and make a name for himself in a manner that was going to get him killed, in a manner that would take away another potential paycheck from the family. She didn't slave over a hot stove every day for eighteen years for her boy to go out and get himself killed. Somebody was going to have to beat some sense into the boy, and she wasn't going to stop her husband from doing just that.

"You're a pathetic coward, and you would never live up to the legacy that your brother left," his father spat the words out in front of his eardrum as his arms squeezed even tighter.

Jones saw stars pop up in his vision as his blood vessels began to pop. He could no longer manage to suck in a breath, and everything began to go black. He kicked out with his feet, trying to knock his father off balance. He managed to do so only briefly, but it was all he needed.

They turned slightly, and Jones saw the beer bottle that his father had drank during supper still next to his plate.

He took his hands off his father's arm and reached for the bottle, managing to get his fingertips around the neck. There was still some liquid inside, and Jones felt it slosh around in the bottle. The cold condensation around the outside of the bottle felt good in his hands compared to the hot flesh around his throat, and he feared how it made him feel having the bottle in his hands after watching it never leave his father's.

Using the last bit of energy he had, he swung the bottle in an upward arc, hoping to hit something.

There was a crunch, and his nose was met with the foul smell of alcohol as he fell to the ground.

Chapter Five

Jones opened his eyes, realizing that there were no longer hands around his throat. He tried to get up, before remembering that he hadn't taken a breath in what felt like forever. He took in a deep breath of air, inhaling the familiar smell of steak and potatoes. He pressed his forehead to the cold tile floor, willing the air to go into his lungs faster.

Then everything started coming back to him.

He had swung the beer bottle, had he hit something?

In his peripheral vision, he could see shards of glass around him on the floor, and his clothes were soaked in beer. He could now smell that the air he breathed in was tainted with the smell of Schlitz, as well as something else, something coppery. Was that blood?

Jones looked to his right and saw his father passed out on the floor. His eyes were closed, and he had obviously been knocked out, as Jones could hear him snoring from his perch on the floor nearby.

His father's head was dripping blood from where Jones had hit him with the bottle, and his mother was crouched over the man, cradling his head in her hands like he was on his deathbed. Jones's mother was crying, begging her husband to wake up, as she rocked him back and forth.

Jones wasn't a doctor, but he could clearly see that his father would be fine, fortune seemed to favor the drunk and stupid.

His mother paid no mind to him as he tried to stand up, it wasn't like he had almost died himself a second ago.

"Ma... Ma!" Jones yelled, trying to get his mother's attention.

She stopped her rocking only for a second, long enough to look up at him with red eyes, her cheeks puffed up as tears ran down her face.

"Get out, and don't you come back to this house, ya hear?" his mother said through gritted teeth. "GET OUT!"

Jones stepped back, holding his chest. The force of her words hit him like a semi-truck.

He could feel the tears rush down his cheeks but didn't have the energy to wipe them away. He just knew that he had to leave, to go somewhere, anywhere but here.

He grabbed the door handle and ran out into the rain, the open door frame acting as a beacon, letting enough light through to show him the way out.

Chapter Six

Jones could still remember the day the Army Officers came to the door. He was sitting on the floor in his room, playing with a die-cast metal toy plane model that he had nicked from his brother's room while he was away.

Suddenly, there was a knock at the door.

One of the reasons that Jones remembered that day so well was because of the silence that followed. Every day in that house was filled with a constant stream of yelling and cursing, of dishes being washed in the sink, or the game playing on the radio, blasting at a rate that was loud enough to drown out his father's surroundings.

There was a knock at the door, and every set of eyes in the house turned to look.

Jones stopped playing with his plane.

His mother turned off the running water in the sink.

His father turned the knob on his radio set and ashed out the cigarette in his hand.

He had never seen that look on his father's face before.

It was one of confusion, mixed with a little bit of fear.

His parents looked at each other, as if silently sending a message between them, asking if the other had invited anyone over.

That was one of the reasons why they were so surprised to hear the knock at the door. They weren't the friendliest family. They never invited anyone over. The Jepsen family tended to enjoy their time away from the general public as much as possible, and the general public felt the same way about them.

Everyone in the neighborhood could hear them yelling at each other through the thin walls of their home, and none of their neighbors dared look their way, let alone knock on their door.

In all the time that Jones had been alive, he had never seen someone approach their front door who wasn't family.

His father leaned over in his seat and peered through the closed curtains on the window, not wanting to make his presence known in case the Jehovah's Witness were outside.

Another look of confusion passed over his face, and the man got out of his recliner to answer the door, not even bothering to put his pants on.

His mother dried off her hands on a dish towel and made her way slowly toward the door as well.

There was another brief knock on the door before Jones's father swung it open.

On the other side of the entranceway stood two officers, both dressed in their full dress blues. One of them still had his hand outstretched to knock on the door.

He lowered it slowly to his side, regaining his composure and straightening his posture.

"May I speak with Daniel Jepsen?" one of the officers asked. He was younger than the other man and appeared to be in his late twenties. He did all the talking, while the older gentleman stood straight with his chin held high. It was as if he was there for no other reason than to witness the fact that the conversation had been carried out.

"That would be me," Jones's father said.

Jones was still on the floor in his room, and therefore unable to see his father's expression.

The officers proceeded to remove their hats and placed them over their hearts.

"The Secretary of the United States Army has asked me to express his deep regret that your son, Private Steven Jepsen, was killed in action last week in Korea. Steven and his platoon marched into an ambush, and though they fought a brave battle, none of them made it out alive."

The words had barely left the young man's mouth before Jones's father hit the floor.

Jones was pretty sure that they had said some other things. In fact, he could distinctly remember seeing their mouths moving, but he couldn't hear any words coming out.

His father, the proud man who could stare down a speeding train without blinking, had collapsed to the floor and started to cry.

His mother was crying too, and his father had shoved his face into the bottom of her dress and was openly weeping into it.

He had never seen his father express any emotion other than anger, so this was a first for him.

Jones couldn't quite understand the fact that his brother had died and that he would never see him again.

The funeral happened a few days later.

The whole family was there, all dressed in black.

Even Aunt Debby showed up. Jones hadn't seen her since she and his father got into an argument a few years ago.

A group of soldiers dressed in uniform carried his brother's casket, which was draped in an American flag.

Jones's mother kicked him and told him to sit up straight after she found him playing with leaves on the ground.

The men placed the casket down, and the ceremony began.

A man that Jones didn't know spoke kind words about his brother, and his father stared straight ahead, never looking at a single person the whole time.

After that man had finished speaking, an army officer presented a flag folded in the shape of a triangle to Jones's father.

"Your son was a good man. You have my deepest condolences," the officer said.

Jones's father just nodded his head, never looking at the man.

The soldiers all stepped to the side, raised up their rifles, and fired several times into the clouds.

Jones just looked into the sky, trying to see what they were shooting at.

They dropped their guns to their sides, then spun around and marched out of the cemetery as the casket slowly descended into the grave.

People threw roses in the hole, and his mother motioned for Jones to stand up, and they too went and dropped flowers on his casket.

Jones looked up at his father, and he watched the man's eyes as he limped over to the hole in the ground. For the first time, they left the sky as the rose left his fingertips and fell onto his son's casket.

Then he turned and walked home.

Jones's father never looked at him that day. He didn't look at him for several weeks after.

It was as if his only son had died that day, as if Jones didn't even exist, as if he wasn't worthy of the Jepsen name his brother left behind.

Chapter Seven

The rain was freezing, and it pelted Jones like a bully with a slingshot on a playground.

He didn't seem to notice as it soaked through his clothes, which now clung to his body like a bag with the air sucked out of it.

Jones walked at a brisk pace down the sidewalks of Briarwood, not sure where he was going, and not caring either. All he knew was that he had to get away from that house, as far away as he possibly could.

He had hoped that he would be able to do just that in the army.

He would be able to fly overseas to a different country and not have to look over his shoulder for his father everywhere he went.

Maybe he could have grown big and strong during boot camp and killed a bunch of Vietnamese soldiers. Then he would come back to town as a hero, and everyone would know his name. Maybe they would throw a parade for his return and put his name in the newspapers. He had hoped that going to the army and making a name for himself and the Jepsen family would make his parents proud and that his father may even want to share a beer with him.

He hated his father more than anyone on the planet, but for some reason, he also craved the man's respect.

But that was over now.

He didn't give a damn what his father or his mother thought from now on.

He kept thinking back to the image of his mother cradling his father on the ground as if Jones wasn't also injured. He could have died, and a mother was supposed to protect her children, yet she had just sat and watched it all happen. Then she had the nerve to go to the man who had hurt her son, who had hurt her in the past.

But that was the last time he was going to worry about his parents or what they thought about him. He was never going back to that house. He didn't know what he was going to do, or where he was going to go, but he knew that there was no place for him there anymore.

He didn't have any family left in Briarwood that would take him in, and he didn't have any friends who he was close enough to that he would be able to ask to crash at their house.

He did have Peggy though.

His mood lifted instantly as he thought of his girlfriend.

Jonah thought about the way her eyes lit up as she looked at him, how her smile could brighten any room the moment she walked in.

Peggy came from the same kind of family that he did. Not abusive or suffering from alcoholism, but they were definitely a much lower class than the rest of the people in town. How her parents managed to create a daughter as beautiful as she was beyond him.

He sometimes lay awake at night and wondered if that was the reason that she was with him. Was it that her parent's insecurities that lowered her standards to the point where she would accept a date from anyone, including Jones?

He brushed the thought out of his mind as he changed course.

He had a new direction in mind, he would stop by Peggy's house.

Jones didn't know what to say to her yet, but he knew that if there was one person on this earth who could brighten up his mood, it would be Peggy.

He turned the corner onto her street, picking up speed as the thought of her made him forget about how cold the rain felt on his skin.

The thought of her was like the first sip of alcohol after a long day, warming him up from the inside out.

He had always dreamed of spending his life with Peggy, but he dreamed of coming back from the war and proposing to her then. But what was stopping him now?

A new thought occurred to him now.

What was waiting for either of them in Briarwood? A life of being society's wastebasket? Treated like they were lower-class scum?

What if they ran away together? Tonight, while everyone else was sleeping. He would knock on her window and convince her to go away with him, free to go anywhere they wanted, to do anything they wanted.

Jones sped up at the thought of this.

He was so focused on his thoughts that he didn't see the strange car parked a few houses down from Peggy's house.

Chapter Eight

Jones could see her house now, which was pretty impressive considering it was dark and raining, and every house looked exactly the same.

But Peggy's house was an image that he had pictured over and over in his head every night for months, even before he asked her to go steady with him.

Deep down, he knew he had always loved Peggy.

Even before he first laid eyes on the girl, he felt that there was an attraction that pulled them together, destined to find each other in the end.

He had first seen Peggy at school one day.

Her parents had just moved into town, with her father managing to secure a job at the local brick factory. It was Peggy's first day of school, and she walked through the front doors clutching her books with her head hung low. She had bad self-esteem issues from her parents and didn't think too highly of her looks. That combined with the fact that she was in a new school where she didn't know anybody and had no friends, Peggy was feeling lost and undesirable.

Jones had spun around from his locker just in time to see her, and as she looked up from the ground for the first time that day, her eyes locked onto his, and it was like magic.

Something just clicked in Jones's head and just like a near-death experience, he saw his life flash before his eyes.

Except it wasn't just his life.

It was theirs.

He could see himself taking this girl out to dance, asking her father for her hand, bringing kids into this world, and playing catch with them in the front yard as she looked on.

All of this happened in his mind in a flash and he knew that he needed to introduce himself.

Jones ran right up to Peggy, a little too closely, causing her to stop dead in her tracks, flustered.

"I wanted to be the first person to meet you, so, hi I'm Jones. Jones Jepsen."

Jones stuck out his hand for her to shake, and she stuck out her own, causing her to drop all her books on the floor.

They both bent down at the same time to pick them up.

"Allow me to grab these for you," Jones said, before looking up to meet her eyes once more.

Jones froze, her eyes making him forget how to breathe.

"Uh, I never got your name," Jones said catching himself,

"That's because I never gave it to you," Peggy said, picking herself up off the ground. Now that Jones was carrying her books, she had a free hand to shake, so she stuck it out to him. "My name is Peggy Myers."

"It's a pleasure to meet you," Jones said, struggling to balance the books in one arm and shake her hand with the other.

Peggy laughed at the struggle she was causing him, and his face went as red as a tomato.

But there was something calming about her smile as she laughed.

He was thinking about her smile when he rounded the corner of her fence, pausing at the edge of her driveway.

He took a moment to catch his breath, thinking of what he would say to Peggy.

Some of the lights were on in her house, and Jones watched through the window as Peggy's mother walked out of the kitchen into the living room with two glasses of wine, then bent over to hand one to Mr. Myers.

He watched as her parents chatted by the fire, laughing and joking without a care in the world.

He was envious of the love those two had for each other, and he strived to be like that one day with their daughter; happy no matter what their circumstances were, as long as they had each other.

Peggy wasn't allowed to have anyone over after dark, so Jones knew that he had to act quickly while her parents were distracted.

He stuck one long leg after another over the fence, careful not to rip his trousers. Then he bent low as he walked toward the side of the house, trying not to be seen in the light coming from the living room window.

Jones saw that the light was on in Peggy's room.

He crouched as he moved towards it, then held onto the window sill as he peered over the top into the room.

There she was, his forever girl.

She was as beautiful as the day he met her, dressed for bed in a flattering gown that accentuated her body.

He found his eyes begin to drift across her, taking in the sight of her with ravenous hunger.

Jones looked down at the grass beneath him. He felt ashamed of feeling this way. He was not a peeping tom and he wouldn't subject his girl to something like that.

He had a mission that he came here to do; get Peggy and go.

Jones raised his fist to the glass, planning to knock just loudly enough to get her attention, but not loud enough for her parents to come running.

He drew his hand back, about to knock when he caught movement out of the corner of his eye.

Jones dropped his hand and ducked his head slightly so he wouldn't get caught by whoever was walking into the room.

This wouldn't be a good look for him if Peggy's father were to see him staring into his daughter's room.

As he peeked over the edge of the window, a figure walked out of the bathroom and into Peggy's bedroom.

It wasn't either of her parents.

Chapter Nine

Jones wiped the drops of rain out of his eyes, sure that he wasn't seeing right. The person in Peggy's room was Robby Fletcher.

He stood well over six feet tall, ruggedly handsome, and was the captain of the football team. If the guy couldn't get any more perfect, he was also the mayor's son, so he pretty much got whatever he wanted.

Robby's father was the mayor not because he wanted to change Briarwood for the better. No, that would be too simple. His father was the mayor because he craved power and liked to loom it over the people whom he wanted to take advantage of.

The mayor stayed in a place on the outside of town, in the biggest house for miles. He didn't get that huge house by being the mayor. No, he got that house from being absolutely loaded. Not only was he the mayor, but he was the owner of the brick factory that employed everyone in town, and he provided the bricks for every house built in the area.

As the mayor, he was able to strike down any attempts to open businesses that would compete with his own.

Robby, being the son of the mayor and the richest man in town, got whatever he wanted, whenever he wanted it.

He once got a teacher to change his grades by threatening to call his father. That day two plus two apparently did equal five.

Jones stared through the glass of his girlfriend's window, wondering what the hell was going on.

Was he at the wrong house?

No, this was too shabby of a home to belong to Robby's family, and besides, he was looking right at Peggy.

Was she tutoring him?

Psht. If Robby needed better grades in school, one call from his father could have the place named after him.

Then why...

Jones lost his train of thought as Robby took his shirt off, exposing a six-pack set of abs that went along with his perfect tan.

Robby threw his shirt to the ground, then motioned for Peggy to come closer.

No, no, no, no, Jones mouthed through the glass.

Peggy got out of bed and pranced over to Robby, who cradled her into his arms.

She put a finger to her lips, then smiled up at him, the same smile that she had used when she looked at Jones.

Robby flashed his million-dollar smile right back at her.

As Jones looked on in horror, Robby bent down and placed his lips on Peggy's.

Jones felt his world crumbling around him. That was HIS girl. Peggy was supposed to be the girl that he married, that he had kids with, and that he would spend the rest of his life with.

Peggy was the girl of his dreams, the one thing he had going for him. And now the one thing he had left had just been taken away from him by the guy who already had everything.

He watched as Robby slowly pushed the straps of her nightgown to the side, and the skimpy outfit fell to the floor in a heap.

Jones couldn't watch any longer.

He stood there, rooted to the spot, unable to look away, but he couldn't see anymore because his eyes had become blurry as they filled with tears once again.

Jones closed his eyes and started to back away, shaking his head as he did so. He tried to shake the memory of what he just saw from his mind. He wanted to pretend that what he had just seen had never happened, so he could go on living the way he was supposed to, but he knew he couldn't do that.

He backed away until he felt the fence behind him. He felt like he had been standing for hours, and with the fence behind him he felt the energy just sap right out of him and he fell to the ground against it, openly weeping into his palms.

Just then, a car drove by, its headlights passing over him giving him a split-second notice before it drove through a nearby puddle. The result was a wave of filthy mud water splashing all over him.

Jones barely noticed.

At this point, somebody could have lit his body on fire and he would have seen it as an improvement over how his day had gone so far.

Jones cradled his face in his hands, adding his tears to the already rain-soaked earth. His long hair, which was normally gelled up and toward the back of his head, now hung around his face, hiding it in shadow. He knew that when he left for the army, he would be forced to keep a buzz cut, so he decided to grow it out as long as he could before he would be made to wear the uniform cut of a soldier. He was thankful for his hair now, as it blocked out the rest of the world and gave him a place to be himself.

He couldn't believe what he had just seen.

Robby knew that Peggy was Jones's girlfriend. Why would he go after her?

Deep down, Jones knew it was because she didn't belong to him, and rich kids like Robby always wanted more than they were given.

Robby was built like a Greek god, with a chin that could cut glass.

He could have his way with any of the girls from school, and from what Jones heard, he did.

Peggy was far from the prettiest girl in school, Robby just wanted her because he hadn't had her yet, and he knew Jones could do nothing to stop him.

But Jones knew that it took two to do what he saw through her window tonight.

Jones tried to tell himself that he didn't know why Peggy would cheat on him, but the answer was obvious.

Peggy came from nothing, her parents having moved to this town to try to create a better life for themselves. Anyone who tends to come from nothing also tends to spend their days trying to increase their quality of life.

Peggy wasn't going to find that with Jones. If anything, the combination of their families would only result in the creation of Briarwood's first trailer park.

No, he knew why she would go for Robby.

Robby had everything that she wanted. A nice house, money, and boundless opportunities. Peggy's family struggled, but with Robby, she wouldn't have to struggle anymore.

But what she didn't know was that Robby tended to treat girls like they were special, like they were everything to him, like he wanted to spend his future making them happy. But after Robby got what he wanted, which was usually just to get into their pants, Robby would leave them high and dry and wondering why they weren't good enough.

Jones didn't want Peggy to feel like she wasn't good enough, because she was good enough.

For him.

Chapter Ten

Jones screamed into his hands, letting the sound of the rain quell the animalistic drones coming from his throat. He no longer had a family that loved him, or a girlfriend waiting on him. There was nothing left for him in this town, and it was all because Robby wanted to have a late-night fling.

Jones's tears of sadness turned into cries of anger, as he clenched his fists, trying to find something to do with this pent-up energy coursing through his veins.

He didn't have to wait very long.

There was a sound coming from the house.

Jones looked up from where he sat in the corner of the yard and saw Robby crawling out of Peggy's window.

Robby must have had his fill of Peggy and decided it was time for him to leave, there was nothing left for him there.

Jones watched as Robby snuck towards the edge of the driveway, looking back toward the house to make sure he wasn't seen by Peggy's parents. No movement came from the direction of the Meyer household.

If he had been looking in the other direction, he might have seen Jones if it weren't so dark and rainy that night.

Jones saw the object of his rage walking toward him and knew what he had to do.

Robby got to the edge of the fence and hopped over it, just feet from where Jones sat.

Jones decided to go after Robby, quietly climbing the fence after him. He followed him down the street until they got to his car, which he had parked a few houses down in order to not be seen by Peggy's parents.

Robby opened the car door, got in, and put the car in neutral, before getting out and shoving the car. As the car picked up speed, he jumped in and shut the door.

Unbeknownst to Robby, Jones had used this time to crawl through the open window on the other side and into the back seat.

When the car was about ten houses from Peggy's, Robby turned the key in the ignition, making the car roar to life. He put it in drive and set it in the direction of his own house.

He had come into town to do something... or someone, and had accomplished his goal. Now it was time to sleep it off in his own bed, away from the lower-class people who lived on Bleeker Street.

What he didn't know was that Jones was in the backseat, covered by Robby's letterman jacket.

Jones was huddled in the space where someone's feet would go, next to the spot where Robby was currently storing his football cleats, the smell of which was giving Jones a run for his money not to wretch in.

The main thing that was helping his cause was his seething, red-hot anger.

Robby reached for the dashboard, spinning a knob that turned on the radio, then cranked it up as loud as it could go.

Through Robby's jacket, Jones could hear today's hits begin to play on 91.7 FM.

Robby smacked his hands on the steering wheel, biting his lip and closing his eyes as he jammed out to a tune on the radio.

Either he was really into the song or he was still buzzing over his night with Jones's girlfriend because Robby rolled down the window and began to howl like a wolf.

"Ow, ow, owooo!" Robby screamed into the night.

Jones's rage felt like it was peaking, and he began to lift his head, trying to figure out the best way to end Robby's life. Looking around, he had an idea.

He rose up from the backseat, the noise of the radio blasting so loud that Robby didn't hear a thing.

In his hands, Jones clutched a shoelace that he had pulled from one of Robby's cleats. His plan was to wrap it around the boy's throat, yanking it back against the headrest until his body ceased to struggle and grew limp.

Yes, they would probably crash, and they could probably both die in the process. But Jones had nothing left to live for, and he would gladly meet Robby in hell.

A pair of headlights washed over the car, and Jones ducked out of instinct.

His heart was beating fast, and he was just given another chance to think about what he was doing.

Would he go through with this?

Suddenly his head slammed against the back of the passenger seat as Robby stepped on his brakes.

They had arrived at the estate that Robby called his home.

Robby shut the car off and got out, leaving Jones alone in the car behind him.

Jones clutched his chest, his heart was racing with adrenaline. He took a deep breath, not remembering whether he was holding it so he wouldn't be heard or so he wouldn't have to smell Robby's cleats.

He peeked over the window to see Robby go inside.

Jones had to get out of the car.

Quietly, he pulled the handle, which subsequently made a loud thud as the lock disengaged.

Jones silently cursed whoever invented automobiles. He didn't own one himself, mostly because he couldn't afford one.

He waited to see if anyone was going to come outside to check on the noise, but nobody did.

It was a peaceful town, where nothing ever happened and people tended to leave their doors unlocked. Plus, people this rich didn't feel like they could be harmed, like they were invincible.

Jones got out of the car, and then started to close the door before realizing that it would make another bang. He wouldn't make the same mistake twice, plus, he wouldn't mind if Robby's battery died overnight.

Jones began to walk toward the edge of the property, deeming his mission failed, when he remembered the reason why he came here.

He thought of the memory of Robby kissing his girlfriend, of him caressing her body. He thought of the way that Robby had reached behind Peggy and snapped the clasps of her bra off with ease.

It was like he had done it before a hundred times with a hundred other girls.

It was like this was just another night for him, like Peggy wasn't even special.

Or maybe he had done it so easily because he had done it to Peggy a hundred times before.

Jones thought of all the nights when he had left her house. Had Robby crawled in through the window the moment Jones left? Or was he there the whole time, just waiting in the closet or under the bed, snickering to himself over what a loser Jones was and thinking about what he was about to do to Jones's girlfriend once he left.

Jones turned around and walked back to the house.

Chapter Eleven

He went right up to the front door. It was unlocked. He knew it would be. Every door in this town was kept unlocked every night. Nobody had anything to be afraid of before. Nothing went bump in the night in Briarwood.

Jones's hand froze on the door knob.

There were too many unknown variables should he walk through this door.

First, he didn't have a weapon.

He could have killed Robby with the shoelace in the car when he was sitting down, but standing up Robby was too tall for Jones to pose as a threat with a piece of string.

Secondly, he didn't know what was on the other side of that door. Would it be the family dog? The father? The butler?

Jones's quarrel wasn't with them.

It was with Robby.

Jones slowly took his hand off the handle, careful not to make a sound.

He walked around the side of the house until he found a room with the light on.

It was the living room, and as he peered through the window he watched as Robby walked up to a woman who Jones could only assume was his mother and kissed her goodnight. His father was next, sitting in a very expensive recliner. This man Jones recognized as the mayor of Briarwood. He tended to show up to every event and act like he had a big part in it. Oh, you saved up every penny you've ever made to open a barbershop? The mayor will be there to cut the ribbon and talk about how he was bringing more jobs into the community. It was all a load of crap, and the man passed down the ability to bullshit to his son, who was now bending over to kiss his father on the forehead and say he was going to bed.

Jones walked along the perimeter of the house, following Robby from room to room as he turned the lights on, making his way to his bedroom.

Finally, Robby turned on a light, revealing posters of girls, cars, and baseball players. On his dresser, there sat an endless supply of trophies for sports and academic accomplishments.

As Jones looked in, he noticed that Robby was walking right toward him.

Jones ducked beneath the window, shutting his eyes tight.

Had he been seen?

Had Robby walked over to grab him, to have him arrested for being a peeping tom?

He tried to think of an excuse, of any reason that he should be outside Robby's window tonight. Due to the circumstances, his mind went blank.

He could do nothing more than hold his breath and wait for what was meant to happen as he heard the window above him slide open.

Jones waited.

And waited.

But nothing happened.

Robby didn't grab him, or call out to whoever might be lurking outside his window.

Jones looked up, expecting to see Robby's face looking down at him from the window.

But he wasn't there.

Jones waited several minutes before he dared move again.

Then he slowly slid up, peeking over the window sill.

Robby was on the other side of the room undressing.

It was an unseasonably hot night, and he had just opened the window to get some air.

Robby got undressed down to his underwear and then walked into the bathroom. A moment later, Jones heard the shower turn on.

He waited until he could hear the water splashing irregularly, meaning that Robby had stepped inside the shower, then Jones made his move.

He reached up and grabbed hold of the windowsill, and pulled himself inside. He made a noise as he hit something on the way down, and he looked toward the shower to see if he had alerted Robby.

Nothing.

The big idiot seemed totally oblivious to his surroundings, completely secure in his environment.

Jones got to his feet, then took a moment to inspect his surroundings.

Robby's room was quite different than his own. Mostly due to the fact that he lived in one of the only custom homes in Briarwood and most of the houses in the area followed the same blueprint. His father had developed the blueprints for all the homes in town, along with supplying the materials for each to be built.

While Jones had one window and a door that led into the hall-way, Robby's room had several windows and doors that led to his own bathroom as well as to other areas in the house. Jones was also pretty sure that his entire house could fit into Robby's room and there would still be space left over.

He took a moment to admire the shelves full of trophies for sporting events and academic achievement, the latter half Jones expected had been paid for by Robby's father as he was sure the boy had taken so many hits to the head in football that he could barely remember his own name.

The rest of the wall space that wasn't taken up by windows or trophy-laden shelves was completely covered in posters of cars and pinup models.

He stopped for a moment to check out a particularly skimpy portrait of Darla Fields wearing nothing but an American flag.

As Jones walked around the room, it was hard not to look at the elephant in the room, the massive king-sized mattress on a four-poster frame. The thing was absolutely huge, and he felt like his whole room could fit on one side of it. The pillows were hotel quality and the duvet was fluffed to the max.

Jones walked over to it and pressed the fabric of the duvet between two of his fingers. It was the softest material he had ever touched in his life.

He couldn't help himself.

He bent his knees and jumped backward, landing on his back on the giant bed.

Jones melted into the duvet, which swallowed him whole. It was like being caressed by a cloud full of angels. As he rubbed his cheeks against the soft fabric around him, he suddenly felt extremely tired.

All of the stress from that day began to catch up with him. The fight with his parents, running through town, all the tears that had left his body. He had been so tensed up and he now felt like he could relax.

As Jones's eyelids began to droop, he noticed a sudden silence in the room.

There was something missing that was just there a second ago.

He couldn't put his finger on it, as he was so relaxed in Robby's bed.

Then it hit him.

The shower had stopped running.

Chapter Twelve

Jones's eyes shot open as he realized that Robby had gotten out of the shower. He tried to get up, but the blanket was all around him, threatening to suffocate him where he lay.

Finally, he was able to free himself, jumping from the bed.

He looked around, trying to see where Robby was, but he hadn't come out of the bathroom yet.

The door was cracked open slightly, and through it, Jones could see Robby checking himself out in the mirror as he brought a comb through his hair.

In all of his comfort while he was lying in Robby's bed he had almost forgotten what he had come here to do.

He had come here to kill Robby.

Jones tiptoed as quietly as he could towards the door.

He stood behind it, unsure of what his next move should be.

He reached for the door handle but paused before opening it.

How would he kill Robby? Beat him to death? The guy was twice his size and could probably bench-press his body. No, Jones wouldn't be able to beat him in hand-to-hand combat. Was there a weapon in the bathroom that he could use to his advantage? Not likely, and he had never heard of anyone being killed with a plunger before.

As his hand hovered over the door handle, it began to turn.

Robby was coming out of the bathroom.

Jones threw himself against the wall as quietly as he could, holding his breath so that he wouldn't be heard.

The door swung open in front of him, blocking him from being seen by Robby.

With the door in front of him, all he could see were the shadows of Robby's feet as he walked through the door. The excess steam from the hot shower flowed out of the open door, filling the room with a shroud-like mist.

Jones could feel his heart beating out of his chest. He felt like it was loud enough that Robby could hear it, and he was going to be caught because of it.

He couldn't see anything from behind the door. For all he knew, Robby could be on the other side of it, waiting for Jones to slip up, to make a sound so he could kick his ass.

He heard the sound of a drawer opening.

Robby must be getting dressed for bed, Jones thought. He must not know that Jones was there.

He felt himself relax a little before he remembered that he was stuck behind a door and the way out was blocked by the person whose room this belonged to.

Jones suddenly felt something dripping down his leg. He was too afraid to move, to look down and see what it was for fear of making a sound and alerting Robby to his presence. Had he pissed himself? He felt like he would have known if he had pissed himself.

That's when he realized that he had been sitting outside in the rain less than an hour ago. All of his clothes were still soaking wet from the rain and from when that car had splashed him.

Had he left a trail?

Would Robby see it and follow it to the back of the bathroom door?

That's when Jones heard the sound of the comforter being moved.

"What the..." Robby said.

Jones had laid in Robby's bed in soaking wet clothes.

For all he knew, there may have been a wet outline of his body on the duvet.

Now Robby had to know that there was someone in his room. He would alert his parents, heck, the authorities and they would come bursting through the door and arrest Jones. Then he would be regaled as the hero who took care of the burglar in Briarwood.

He couldn't let that happen.

He couldn't let that smug son of a bitch get any more credit. Not after he just slept with Jones's girlfriend.

The image of Robby taking off Peggy's bra went through his head once more, and it was all he needed.

Jones felt the blood rush to his head as the surge of anger returned, and he felt the need to do something about it.

On the wall to his right, there was a section of trophies dedicated to when Robby had played in croquet tournaments. And hanging on a rack under the shelves of trophies there was a mallet, normally used to tap balls through hoops on the ground.

Jones seized his chance.

He burst out from behind the bathroom door, ripping the mallet off the wall.

Jones turned to see Robby spin around in fear.

He hadn't expected to see Jones at all.

He had felt the wet comforter and thought he must have sat down after the shower by accident and gotten the blanket wet. Robby had all but gotten comfortable when Jones came after him from out of the dark corner.

Robby tried to scream, but the sound was choked off as Jones hit him in the Adam's apple with a solid swing of the mallet.

Robby let out a sound like a tropical bird as he dropped to all fours, clutching his throat with one hand.

Jones spun the mallet in the air, liking how it felt in his hands. There was a certain weight and balance to it, and he felt like King Arthur handling Excalibur, with a blade crafted specifically for him.

Jones swung the mallet down and back up again, this time cracking Robby in the side and sending him toppling over onto his back.

He may have just broken a couple of his ribs, and Jones didn't think Robby would be playing football anytime soon.

Robby clutched his side with one hand, then stuck the other in the air as if to beg Jones not to hit him again. As he did so, he caught sight of who his attacker was, and his eyes lit up with recognition, then fear.

Robby tried to say something.

Jones looked down at the asshole who stole his girlfriend.

Was he trying to apologize? Was he trying to beg Jones to spare his life?

Jones would never find out, as Robby's voice box had been smashed into next week.

Jones kicked Robby's hand to the ground, then stepped on his wrist. He remembered back to an hour before when Robby had used this hand to undress Peggy.

Another surge of rage moved its way through Jones's body, and he felt the energy course through him as he swung the mallet once more. This time he brought it over his head, building up speed and letting gravity help him out as he brought the hammer end of the mallet down on Robby's hand.

He heard the sound of the bones in Robby's palm break, and he was surprised at how much it sounded like celery being snapped in half.

As Jones pondered this fun fact, Robby squirmed underneath him, trying to rescue his poor hand from under Jones's foot.

Robby was trying to scream in pain, but due to his throat being mangled, the only sound that came out was "curhh, curhh."

As Robby tried to snatch his hand back, Jones dug the heel of his foot deeper into the boy's wrist.

He wasn't done with it yet.

Jones brought the mallet up over his head once more, before bringing it down again and again, crushing each of Robby's fingers until they flopped around like rubber, the bones no longer able to support the weight of his own skin.

Jones removed his heel from Robby's wrist, allowing him to see his mangled hand, the hand which would never touch his Peggy ever again.

Jones enjoyed the look of pure horror that adorned Robby's face as he saw it. The boy would never throw a ball again. He would have to learn to write with a different hand. He would be crippled for the rest of his life.

That is, if Jones were to let him live.

Which of course, he couldn't let that happen.

The moment he walked out of this house, Robby would get help and the police would be on Jones in minutes.

No, Robby would have to die.

Robby seemed to come to this conclusion as well, as he fought to get up from the ground and run away. But it was hard to do that with one hand, and as he tried to push himself up, Jones hit the elbow of his other arm with the mallet.

With a sickening crunch, Robby's elbow bent in the wrong direction.

Robby fell to the floor, writhing in pain. He let out a silent scream, one that his parents would never hear.

But something seemed to come over Robby then. Something that Jones didn't expect.

When a person feels like they may be on the verge of death, a sort of animalistic will to survive overtakes them, and a newfound energy courses through them where they will do anything to live.

Jones was learning so many new things tonight.

As he watched, Robby tried to get up again, to make one last attempt to escape.

He got up on all fours once more, putting his weight on his broken fingers, and somehow managed to stand up.

Jones was almost impressed.

But then Robby stood over him, at least two heads taller than Jones.

Robby debated whether to run to safety or to turn and try to fight Jones.

Being that he was a stupid jock on the football team, he thought that his size might give him an advantage, and he didn't want Jones to be able to escape.

He made the mistake of turning toward Jones, putting all his weight behind him as he ran at him.

Jones stared as Robby came at him, useless arms flailing at his sides. His eyes were bloodshot with fear and anger, like an animal with nothing left to lose.

Except he did have something to lose.

When he was about a foot away from Jones, he swung the mallet, low this time, breaking Robby's kneecap and sending him into the wall.

There was a loud clatter as trophies fell off the wall, hitting the floor and shattering almost as badly as Robby's kneecap just did.

Jones's ears picked up, and he listened for any sound coming from the house.

Had they just been heard? Would somebody come looking?

He waited a few seconds but turned back when he heard nothing.

"Ha! Your parents don't seem to give a shit about you," Jones whispered to Robby, who was moaning and moving his body around like a worm on the sidewalk after a fresh rain. "You just had to sleep with my girlfriend, didn't you."

He gave Robby a hard kick to the ribs, sending him onto his back once more, he wanted Robby to see what he was doing to him. He wanted to see the pain in his eyes as it all played out, the sense of hopelessness as he realized he was about to die.

"The one thing I had."

Jones brought the mallet down upon his foot.

Robby bit a hole in his lip, drawing blood.

"The one thing I cared about."

He swung the mallet down on Robby's calf.

Robby slammed his hand onto the ground in pain, which in turn only caused him more pain.

"I was going to ask Peggy to marry me."

The mallet hit Robby in the stomach.

Robby's face turned blue as he got the wind knocked out of him. He tried as hard as he could, but he couldn't manage to suck in a breath.

"But you took that from me because you had to have everything."

With that, Jones brought the mallet down again and again and again.

He let out all of the pent-up rage he had toward Robby, Peggy, and his family. All of the anger came out and was released on Robby until every inch of his body was pulverized.

Jones watched as the light left Robby's eyes.

He didn't want to give Robby the sweet release of death, like a deer that you put down after hitting it with your car.

No, he wanted Robby to feel every bit of pain up until his last breath.

He wanted his face to be the last one that Robby saw before he died.

Jones stood over the body of the man who helped ruin his life, and a grin spread across his face.

Chapter Thirteen

"Robby? Are you alright?" Came a voice from down the hall. Jones froze, the murder weapon still in his hands.

He looked around the room, only just realizing that it was covered in Robby's blood.

Jones looked down, his entire outfit which had been soaked with rainwater earlier was now also stained red, a Jackson Pollock painting that proved that he had accomplished what he had set out to do.

He had killed Robby, and the evidence was all over him.

He heard footsteps in the hall, coming closer with every second.

Jones looked around for a place to hide.

The spacious room was devoid of hiding places. What would he do, hide under the bed until the police came?

No, and hiding behind the bathroom door again wouldn't be a sufficient option this time. This space was too big for him to jump out the window in time, he was on the opposite side of the room and the hallway door was between him and the window.

The bathroom!

He heard the door handle begin to turn.

It wasn't much, but it would have to do for now.

Jones ran into the bathroom, closing the door all the way except for a small crack so he could see. He turned the bathroom lights out just in time to hear the door to the hallway swing open.

"Robby?" A woman's voice called out. "Robby, I heard a lot of banging coming from your room, are you alright?"

Suddenly, a piercing scream broke through the night.

"ROBBY! Oh no, Robby, my baby!"

Jones looked through the crack in the door in time to see Robby's mother on the ground, holding her dead son in her hands. Tears streamed down her cheeks as she tried to wake him up, but that wasn't going to happen. Even if she did manage to bring him back to life, he would be in so much pain that he might try to end his own life.

Jones heard more footsteps running through the house, and he assumed Robby's father had heard his wife scream and decided to check it out.

He needed to find a way out of this situation and fast.

Jones saw a light out of the corner of his eye.

He turned around and saw the outline of another doorway behind him.

Quietly, he stepped over to the other door and pushed, hoping that the door wouldn't creak. It didn't, and he never thought he would be so thankful that Robby's family was rich.

The door opened to reveal another bedroom, devoid of occupants. It had been a connecting door with a shared bathroom between the two bedrooms.

Thank god for rich people and their need to have extra unneeded bedrooms, Jones thought to himself.

He closed the door behind him, just in time to hear Robby's father rush into the room next door.

The following screams of anguish alerted him to the fact that the man had seen his dead son.

Jones needed to move.

He scanned the room, looking for a way out.

It was a basic guest bedroom, complete with all the comforts one would need during their visit, such as a bed, dresser, and nightstands, but was otherwise devoid of personality. On the other side of the room, Jones spotted the doorway out.

He tiptoed up to the door, then grasped the cold bronze handle. He stood there, unmoving, trying to will his hand to turn, but it just wouldn't do it. He feared that the mechanism inside would make a sound as the latch sprung free, alerting the Fletcher family to his location.

He reasoned that if he stood still any longer then it wouldn't take much time for them to find him.

Jones took a deep breath, then went for it, closing his eyes as the handle spun in his grasp.

If it made a sound, Jones never heard it.

He had opened the door just a crack when his ears were met with a torrent of sound. It was like he had just stepped into a waterfall, with noise crashing down around him like the waves of a tsunami.

He had been so focused on himself not making a sound that he had forgotten about the sounds of the other people in the house.

"ALISTAIR! PHONE THE POLICE AT ONCE! MY BOY HAS BEEN MURDERED!" The voice of Robby's father bellowed down the hall, assaulting Jones's eardrums as the man called for his butler.

He tried to close off his ears to the mayor's voice, trying to listen for any other sounds happening in the house.

Jones could hear the wailing sounds of Robby's mother, whose crooning began at a quiet whimper and would rise in pitch until it sounded like the pinched mouth of a balloon.

Deeper in the house, he could hear the footsteps of the man named Alistair, presumably on his way to call the police.

He strained his ears, but couldn't hear any other movement in the house.

Jones opened the door ever so slightly, peeking into the hall to see if he would be seen.

At the end of the hall, he could see Robby's open doorway. From where he stood he could just see the legs of the family on the ground.

Robby's mother's feet were shaking as she cried, and the heel of her shoe carved a trail in the carpet next to Robby's own feet, which were noticeably limp and unmoving. His father was shaking the boy's body, trying to wake him up, as if he was only asleep, as if all he needed was to move around a little and the blood would magically find itself back in his body. But that clearly wouldn't happen, and his legs just flopped around lifelessly with the man's efforts.

The boy's parents were too invested in their son's lifeless form to see Jones standing out in the hallway, watching them.

He felt like he must've stood there for hours, staring at the reaction of a family that actually cared about their son, who actually cried at his death. It made him wonder if his parents would cry over him when he was gone. Would they even care? Would they go to his funeral?

That's when Jones noticed the bloody shoeprints that led to the bathroom, which would likely lead to where he was currently standing, and he knew he had to keep going, to find a way out of this massive house without being caught by Robby's family.

Chapter Fourteen

Jones crept back down the hallway, his hand still firmly grasping the wooden mallet, prepared to use it should he encounter any unexpected wanderer in the house. It felt good in his hands, calming even, like it was always meant to be there.

He could hear the butler in the kitchen, talking on the phone with the police.

Keeping his breath calm, he took each step as slowly as he could, walking backward so he could see if someone were to come out of Robby's room. He tested each step before placing the full weight of his foot, making sure he wouldn't step on any creaking floorboards that would alert the family.

He was paying so much attention to his foot placement that he didn't notice the object behind him.

Jones backed into a hat rack, which tumbled to the floor, causing a crashing noise to echo throughout the hall.

He scrambled around, picking up all the hats and placing them back on the rack, trying to disguise the fact that he was there.

Jones placed the last hat on the rack, a black top hat that seemed new, then he listened to see if anyone heard the commotion.

What he heard chilled him to the bone, or at least, what he didn't hear.

There wasn't a sound to be heard in the house, as each of its occupants stopped what they were doing to listen, realizing that they may not be alone, that the killer may still be walking these very halls.

Jones forgot how to breathe, as he played a silent game of chicken with the house's occupants, each waiting for the other to move first.

The butler was the first one with enough stones to do so. As a paid employee of the house, he was the first line of defense for the Fletcher family. If they were to die then he would lose his job. Should he do nothing, then they all could die. He had to check it out, whether he wanted to or not.

Jones's heart began to beat faster as he heard the butler's footsteps growing closer to him.

He looked around, trying to find someplace to hide.

To his left, he saw the front door, with enough locks on it to keep out an army. It would take him forever to get through that. It was time that he did not have. To his right, he saw a coat closet. It may be the first place the man would look, but it was the only thing he had time to do.

Jones swung the closet door open, sliding in between two fur coats before closing the door behind him.

He heard the footsteps grow louder and louder, until suddenly they stopped altogether.

Jones peeked through the slats in the closet door, trying to see what was happening in the hall outside.

The butler had stopped at one of the openings to the hallway, not wanting to barge into the area if the killer really was there. He was quite large, even bigger than Robby had been, and his sleeves struggled to contain the muscles that were threatening to bust through.

Jones guessed that the Fletcher family had hired a butler who could also act as a bodyguard if need be, and with a family as well built as them, they would need to hire somebody even bigger.

The man had stopped in the kitchen to pick up a knife, and was tip-toeing through the hall, searching for the person who had killed Robby.

As Jones watched, the man looked toward Robby's room, where his parents were staring out from his bedroom door, waiting for the butler to handle the problem for them.

The man gestured for them to get back inside the room and close the door, before turning toward the other end of the hall, where Jones stood huddled in the closet.

The butler walked over to the hat rack, noticing that it was slightly awry from where it usually stood. He bent down to pick up a hat that Jones had forgotten, and he placed it at the top of the rack. He looked at the front door, only feet away, and noticed that it was still locked from the inside. The killer couldn't have escaped that way.

Which left...

The butler's eyes glanced over to the closet where Jones was hidden. The man brought the knife up to his waist, pointing it in the direction of the closet.

He took one step forward, then another, carefully biding his time in case someone were to jump out at him.

As he got closer, Jones could make out several details about the man.

The man was bald by choice, and a light stubble grazed the top of his head like a five o'clock shadow. His pinstriped shirt was tucked into his pants and the man's boots looked nicer than anything Jones owned. His eyes were dark brown, and from where Jones stood only inches away, he could see fear behind them.

The butler was reaching for the closet handle, so close that Jones could smell the man's aftershave.

It was quite pleasant, and it was a shame that he was going to have to kill this man.

As the handle turned, Jones tightened his grip on the mallet, ready to leap out and bash the man's brains in with a single thwack. The man hadn't done anything to Jones, but he would do what he had to do to survive.

Suddenly, Jones saw a glimmer of light on the blade of the butler's knife. The man saw it too, and he pulled his hand away from the closet as red and blue lights flashed across his face.

The butler covered his eyes with one hand as he struggled to see through the glass of the front door.

The police had shown up, and the butler went outside to fill them in on what had happened.

As the door closed behind the man, Jones let out all the breath he had been holding.

He needed to get out of there, but now the front door was compromised, and soon the police would be roaming the house, searching for clues as to where he was.

Jones looked down, using the light from the headlights of the police cars to examine his wardrobe. His clothes were covered in Robby's blood, and should he get out of this house alive, he would surely be seen walking down the street covered in red liquid. He needed to cover up his appearance, so he wouldn't be recognized.

Jones searched the closet until he found a fancy velvet trench coat that likely belonged to the mayor. He slipped it on over his bloody t-shirt, and he liked the way it fit his body.

Looking through the slats in the closet door, he checked to see if there was anyone in the hall outside. Seeing no one, he pushed the door open, mapping out his escape.

To his back was the front door, where multiple police officers were currently being briefed on the situation outside. Down the hall, Robby's parents were still huddled in his room. This meant that his only way out would be through the kitchen where the butler had just come from.

Jones picked up the mallet and began to walk towards the

kitchen, but stopped and spun on his heel. He walked back over to the hat rack and plucked the black top hat off the rack.

Palming the top of the cap, he placed it on top of his head, bringing the brim low upon his forehead.

As the red and blue police lights danced across his face, Jones smiled.

Chapter Fifteen

Jones slipped through the kitchen door just as he heard the sounds of the front door knob turning. Any moment now, the police were going to walk through that door and begin searching the place for him. He needed to be long gone before that happened.

The kitchen was equipped with all the tools a chef would need to create any meal the Fletcher family desired. Jones was pretty sure the stove in this place by itself would cost more than his house cost to build.

A pot rack hung from the ceiling above the island, and dozens of pots and pans hung down like mistletoe in a doorway. The island was about ten feet long, and one side was lined with a row of barstools. The fridge was designed to blend in with the cabinets, appearing as a very large wooden door with a gold trim handle. The wall opposite the cabinets was made of a wall of glass, and Jones was sure that it probably provided wonderful views of the backyard, but for now, it was shrouded in the darkness of night.

As Jones searched for a way out, he saw the back door tucked at the other end of the room. He was about to make a run for it when he heard footsteps behind him.

Jones froze, afraid to move a muscle, afraid to turn around and show his face to the police.

As he waited, the footsteps moved away, and Jones realized that they were coming from the hallway, as the police walked to Robby's room to check on the situation.

He needed to be quick.

After seeing Robby's lifeless body lying in a heap in his room, they would likely search the house for clues, and come upon Jones still frozen in the kitchen.

He waited until the footsteps disappeared, then he made a break for the door.

Jones twisted the deadbolt back as slow as he could, to prevent it from slamming back into its housing. Once that was done, he squeezed the handle and turned, his heart beating a mile a minute as he realized he was going to get out of there without getting caught.

As the door inched open, it made the sound of a banshee screaming in the night.

Jones froze once again, waiting for the police to come running into the room. He heard the sound of Robby's door opening, of someone sticking their head out and listening. After a few moments, they went back into the room, but they left the door open.

Jones knew he couldn't leave through the backdoor. The hinges hadn't been oiled recently, and they would definitely alert the police to his presence. He could open it really quickly and run outside, but the police would know where he was immediately and begin to give chase. He wanted to sneak out unseen, without the suspicion that he was still in the house.

Reluctantly, he let go of the door handle, searching for another way out.

Jones walked quietly into the dining room, where he found what he was looking for.

The center of the room contained a large dining table with chairs all around it. Chandeliers hung overhead, and candlesticks graced the center of the table.

That wasn't what he was interested in though.

What caught his eye was the breakfast nook in the corner of the room.

It was a combination of three benches in a U shape around a table. It reminded Jones of sitting at a booth at the local diner. Above the breakfast nook was an open window.

Jones ran over to it as quietly as he could. He could hear the police in Robby's room collecting a statement from the Fletcher family. He didn't have much time.

He stepped onto one of the benches, then pushed the half-open window up the rest of the way, cringing at the slight sound it made when it moved.

Just then, he heard footsteps moving toward his direction, coming from the hall.

Jones panicked, jumping out of the window without knowing what was underneath it.

His body landed on a bush, and he thanked himself for stealing the mayor's coat, which protected him from getting cut up by its branches.

Jones crouched behind the bush, just in time to see the dining room light turn on.

Someone was in the room that he had just occupied.

He held his breath, getting as low as he could to avoid being seen.

Jones heard a sound, and he peeked up through the bush, looking back at the window he had jumped through.

Standing just a few feet from him, peering out of the window, was the chief of police.

Could the man see him?

Jones hoped that it was dark enough outside that he would be hidden from sight.

After a few tense moments, the man moved away from the window, his footsteps dying out as he moved into a different area of the house.

Chapter Sixteen

Jones slunk around the backyards of his neighbor's houses. He had managed to escape the Fletcher house while the police were still inside, and due to the fact that he had gotten there in Robby's car, Jones had to walk all the way home. This normally wouldn't have been a problem, as it was a small town, but Jones was currently covered in the blood of his classmate while dressed in the mayor's clothes. To make matters worse, as he walked, the sun was coming up, slowly illuminating the way home.

He had to be quick, or the whole neighborhood would see him doing the walk of shame away from the scene of a murder and it wouldn't be long before he would end up in a jail cell.

But Jones had a plan. He would cut through everyone's backyards to avoid being seen by those leaving for work for the morning shift at the brick factory.

Then he would sneak into the window of his parents' house, change into something less suspicious, and pretend that he was home the whole time.

He hadn't forgotten about his fight with his parents, or how they kicked him out, but he would deal with that problem when it came.

Jones was almost to his house, as he hopped the fence into the neighbor's yard, he realized he had made a lapse in judgment with how easy this would be.

For one, he had forgotten about the neighbor's dog, Sparky, who happened to be a purebred German Shepard.

Jones normally didn't spend a lot of time in his neighbor's backyard, so he had never spent much time thinking about their dog, or where they kept it.

As Jones's feet hit the ground, he heard a curious whimper coming from the direction of the house.

His head spun to face where the sound had come from, and he saw Sparky pick his head up from where he lay on the back porch. The dog turned its head, as if Jones was a squirrel and was curious what his next move would be.

Jones contemplated what he should do next.

The dog was on the back porch, approximately thirty yards from where he stood. Jones needed to cross the yard to the other fence in order to get into his own yard, which was about twenty feet from where he stood.

Should he make a run for it, crossing the yard, outrunning a German Shepard, and hopping the fence? Or should he go back over the fence from which he had just come and try to find another way home?

Jones weighed out his options as the dog stared him down, willing him to make the first move.

If he were to go back over the fence behind him, the dog would likely still run up to him and bark until the owners came out. This would wake up the whole neighborhood, and it would draw more attention to him as he tried to find another way to his house, and he would get caught. Whereas if he were to cross the yard and hop the fence, even if the dog barked, he would be in his own yard and be able to get into his bedroom without being seen.

Choice number two would be his only option.

He turned his head to look at the dog, getting ready to sprint across the yard. The dog seemed to register this movement, understanding that Jones had made his choice. This would be a showdown for the ages.

Jones sprinted for the fence, his arms pumping as he went. He was on the track team at school, so he was used to running fast, but usually when he ran he wasn't wearing a trench coat and carrying a mallet. This new ensemble was slowing him down, with only the fear of the dog keeping him running at full speed.

The moment Jones lifted his foot to take his first step, Sparky leaped into the air, his leg muscles rippling as he bound across the yard.

The dog's ears pressed back against his head as he went into protection mode. He needed to make his owners aware of this threat, much like he made them aware of the mailman who threatened to break in and kill them with a bundle of letters every day.

Foam dripped from Sparky's mouth as he barked, a ferocious bellow that started off with a growl that came from his diaphragm before erupting passed his jagged fangs. His paws tore into the earth as he moved, kicking up grass as he made his way towards Jones, who had made the mistake of crossing into Sparky's territory.

Jones heard the dog barking and turned to look at him as he ran. This cost him dearly, as he misplaced his next step, and his foot slid on the grass which was soaked in morning dew.

The dog was on him in a second.

Before Jones could get up, Sparky pounced, digging its claws into his chest.

Jones reached up, placing his hands around the dog's throat as the dog attempted to bite his face off.

Sparky barked and growled, only inches from Jones's face. As he did so, drool spewed from its mouth and covered him in slime that smelled like wet dog food.

Jones was pinned to the ground, and in just a few moments, he wouldn't be able to hold the dog off any longer and it would go for his jugular. Even if the dog didn't kill him, its barking would soon wake the neighbors, who would question why he was trespassing in their yard and covered in blood. He needed to act fast.

Jones frantically looked at the ground around him, searching for something that he could use as a weapon against the dog.

There were some chew toys to his left, just out of reach. To his right, he spotted the mallet which he had stolen from the Fletcher house.

He took his right hand off the dog's throat and pushed it away with his left hand. Using his right hand, he reached for the mallet, the dog's weight preventing him from fully extending himself. His fingers just brushed against the wood of the handle, but he wasn't able to get a full grasp on it.

Jones heard movement coming from the house. The neighbors would be getting dressed to come outside and see what their dog was freaking out about.

It was now or never.

Jones used both hands and pushed Sparky off of him with whatever strength he had left.

The dog only moved about two feet, but it was enough.

Jones rolled to his right, grabbing the mallet. The dog rushed toward him again, barking furiously. It opened its mouth to bite Jones and in that moment he shoved the stick end of the mallet into the dog's mouth.

It bit down, not seeming to recognize that the mallet was not a part of the intruder.

Jones let go of the mallet, letting the dog have it as it threatened to chew the thing to bits.

With the dog distracted, Jones took a running start and leaped over the fence, landing with a thud on his side of the yard, just as the neighbor's porch door opened.

Chapter Seventeen

Jones lay silent on the ground, trying to catch his breath. He could hear his neighbor berating the dog for barking this early in the morning and stealing items from the neighboring houses.

He was in the clear with the neighbors at least.

He still needed to get into his house.

Jones walked around to the side of the house, finding the living room window. He peered over the edge of the window and saw that both of his parents were up. His father was sitting in his chair, reading the morning paper, while his mom scrubbed dishes at the kitchen sink across the house.

He figured that with the sound of the sink running, he might be able to get inside without being heard. His plan was to get inside without being heard, change clothes, and then leave before his parents had time to yell at him again.

Jones snuck around to the back of the house where his room was situated. He never locked his bedroom window just in case he needed to sneak out, plus nobody had ever broken into a home in Briarwood.

Jones 1963

Until last night, Jones thought to himself.

He pressed his hands to the glass of the window, then slowly pushed it up. Using a cement block that he had placed below the window for the specific occasions when he would sneak out, Jones stepped onto the block and over the window frame into his room. What he was not counting on was the fact that he was currently wearing a floor-length trench coat. As he went to bring his other foot through the window, he stepped on the hem of the coat and slipped to the ground.

There was a loud thump as Jones faceplanted onto the floor of his bedroom.

From the other room, he heard his father yell "What the hell was that?"

Jones scrambled to his feet as the sound of the springs in his father's chair groaned, announcing that his father had stood up. He moved back toward the window, contemplating escape, but he knew his parents would catch him crawling out of the window. There wasn't enough time to escape, he had to think of another plan.

Quickly, Jones took off the trench coat and threw it out the window. Then he stripped down to his underwear and shoved the rest of his bloody clothes out the window before slamming it shut.

Just then, the door opened behind him.

He spun around just in time to his father's angry face coming through the door. In his hand, he held a Louisville slugger, a wooden bat which if swung correctly could have the power to remove his head from his shoulders.

As Jones stood there in his skivvies, waiting for his father to get revenge on him for hitting him the night before, he squeezed his eyes shut. He waited for the blows to come, but they never did. He opened one eye, just in time to see the bat fall from his father's hands.

It clattered to the ground, and his father did something he had never done before.

He hugged Jones.

Jones stood there, with his arms pinned to his sides, wondering what the hell was happening.

How hard had he hit his father?

As he stood pondering this question, his father called out for his mother to come into the room.

"It's okay to come in. It's Jones!" his father yelled.

His mother came into the room and likewise hugged him, a single tear running down her cheek.

"We're so glad you're okay!" his mother cried into his shoulder.

This was not the reaction he was expecting.

"Ummm, okay..." Jones said, the confusion clear in his voice.

His parents pulled back from him, noting the awkward tension that had entered the space between them.

His mother took a deep breath, looking back at his father as if she was figuring out a way to tell him something.

"Jones, I'm going to need you to sit down for this," his mother said.

They sat down on the edge of his bed, and his mother stole another look at his father. They must have sent a silent message between each other, because he promptly left the room.

"Jones, I hate to tell you this, but there is a murderer on the loose in Briarwood." His mother stared at him, and he realized that she was waiting for his reaction.

"Oh, um, how do you know? Who did they kill?" Jones asked, pretending like he didn't know what was coming next.

His mother seemed like she was unsure of how to proceed, but just then his father entered the room carrying today's newspaper.

"Uhh, here you go," his father said, shoving the paper into Jones's hands.

Jones spun the paper around until it was facing the correct direction.

On the front page, in bold letters, it read: ***Mayor's Son Murdered In Cold Blood,***
Killer Still On The Loose!

Chapter Eighteen

Beneath the title, there was a side-by-side image. To the left was one of Robby's school photos. He looked perfect in every way. A chiseled jaw, movie star smile, and not a hair out of place. He looked ready to run for president, and with a photo like that, Jones was sure he would have won.

To the right of Robby's school photo, there was a much different image. The photo was taken from the hall of the Fletcher household. The hall which Jones had been creeping down only hours earlier.

The photo showed Robby's open door, and inside you could only see Robby's feet, which were covered under a stained white sheet.

The image was in black and white, but the real thing was still very much imprinted on his mind, and he could still see red everywhere he looked.

As he studied the image, his parents gave each other a look, as if wondering what to do next. If they had still been looking at Jones, they may have seen the corner of his mouth tick up into a smile briefly. When his mother looked back at him, he had replaced his smile with a look of mock concern.

"I know Robby was your friend, Jones."

He was not.

"And I know that you are shocked by this news."

Once again, he was not, although he was a little shocked that it had made it to the papers already.

"But I can assure you that the police are doing everything they can to catch the killer. If you need anyone to talk to, our door is open."

If there was one thing that Jones was sure of, it was that his parents wouldn't know a thing to say if he were to come to them for help. In fact, when his brother died in the war, they had all but shut him out completely.

But as his parents left the room, a tiny switch in his brain flipped. He had just killed somebody, and he had enjoyed it. Instead of being punished for what he had done, his parents appeared to treat him better for it.

Jones looked up as his mother poked her head back into his room.

"Put on something nice, we're going to the town hall. One of the things they mentioned in the article was that the town was going to have a meeting about all this," his mother said. She gave him another look, then closed the door behind her.

Jones walked up to the mirror and wiped a drop of blood from under his collar line, then he smiled.

Chapter Nineteen

A crowd of people had gathered outside the town hall by the time that Jones and his parents had arrived.

Some people were crying, holding handkerchiefs to their eyes as they mourned the town's golden boy. Others sat on the steps and smoked as they processed the fact that a murder had happened right under their noses.

A few people moved aside as the Jepsen family made their way to the town hall doors. They were dressed in their best Sunday clothes, trying to appear respectful to Robby and his mourning family.

The Jepsens opened the door to the town hall and were surprised to see that the town hadn't waited until the allotted time to start the meeting. The townspeople were up in arms and weren't going to wait to be told when to speak, so the town officials elected to start earlier.

The Jepsens sat down just in time to hear their neighbor stand up and ask a question.

"Is there a killer on the loose?" Mr. Livingston asked.

Several people in the room piped up, agreeing with the question at hand.

Jones looked around, noting that it seemed like the whole town was there. His family had grabbed some of the last seats available, and people were still streaming in and standing along the walls.

Toward the front of the crowd, he could see Robby's friends huddled together. Max, Kyle, and Carol stood side by side, their faces red with tears.

Jones smirked, then hid it with a cough before anyone could see him.

At the front of the room, there was a large table where all of the elected officials sat, minus the mayor who appeared to be absent, and for good reason. If there was ever a time to call out of work, it would be the day when your son becomes the first murder victim the town has ever known.

Surrounding the mayor's empty seat, the rest of the officials leaned in together to discuss how much they should tell the town. They didn't want to say too much and send the town into a panic, but they also didn't want to say too little and have people brush off the fact that there was a murderer on the loose.

One of the men closest to the center of the table cleared his throat, then began to address the crowd.

"Yes, there is a killer amongst us," he said.

The crowd began to murmur amongst themselves. Not paying much attention to the men at the front of the room.

The chief of police, Frank DeSalvo, who stood in front of the table, blew his whistle, which emitted an ear-piercing screech that echoed across the walls of the town hall.

Jones covered his ears, just as many of the people around him did the same.

The room grew silent, and the man at the table nodded at the officer.

"Thank you. Yes, it appears that last night someone snuck into the Fletcher household and took the life of dear Robby Fletcher. Police arrived at the scene soon after, but were unable to locate the culprit. This means that there is a killer walking around out there."

Some of the people in the crowd began to look around, as if the killer was going to present himself to them.

Jones felt himself shrinking in his seat, trying not to be seen.

He didn't feel bad about taking Robby's life, but he also didn't want to go to prison for it.

"We will track down the person responsible for Robby Fletcher's death, and we will punish them to the fullest extent of the law."

A man stood up in the center of the crowd. Jones recognized him as the local veterinarian.

"You're telling me that you have no idea who killed him?" the veterinarian said.

Another person stood up in the back.

"There is a murderer walking around Briarwood and you just expect us to go about our day like nothing happened?"

A door opened behind the table, and the crowd grew hushed once more as Mayor Fletcher walked into the room.

The rest of the men at the table stood up and offered him their condolences.

The mayor shook each of their hands before insisting that they have a seat. He then walked over to where he normally sat at the table and gripped the back of the chair.

"I know you're all scared," the mayor began, "Hell, I'm scared. My boy got murdered under my roof while I was in the house."

Some of the people in the crowd looked down, afraid to meet the gaze of the mayor, for fear that doing so may make them burst into tears. The tragedy was still so new to them, as it only happened a few hours ago.

"When I first brought Fletcher Industries to Briarwood, there were only a few houses in the town. But I looked around and I knew that there was greatness in this land, and I believed that we could do great things here. Now I believe wholeheartedly in the Briarwood police department and we will do everything in our power to catch the person responsible for my son's death, and we will try to prevent any of you from feeling what my family is feeling right now. I am willing to provide whatever resources needed to bring this person to justice, starting with a ten thousand dollar reward for anyone with information leading to the arrest of Robby's killer,"

At the sound of Robby's name, the mayor looked down, trying to ward off tears. His grip on the back of the chair was white-knuckled, and when he finally looked back up, his eyes were moist. Without meeting the stares of the people of the crowd, he motioned for the chief of police to come up.

"I believe the chief has something that he wants to tell you," Mayor Fletcher said.

Police Chief Frank DeSalvo lumbered up to the front of the room, watching the mayor the whole while to make sure he was okay. After convincing himself that the mayor wasn't going to do something rash, the chief turned to the people of Briarwood and began.

"There are several protocols that we have to enforce in the event of a murder in our town. Firstly, we must enforce a 9 p.m. curfew starting now until the killer has been captured. We strongly advise that everyone lock their doors and windows every night to prevent this man from getting in. Our department has allotted extra funds to keep every officer we have on staff on duty every night to patrol the streets and keep everyone safe until the moment that this man is caught. We will spare no expense to keep Briarwood safe."

Chapter Twenty

As the town hall meeting drew to a close, rumors began to fly around about who the killer could be.

Was it the postman? He came to everyone's house six days a week. He knew when people would be home, and he knew where all the potential entryways to a house were. After all, he spent his days walking packages to their front doors.

Or was it David Cunningham?

The man was known to drink passed his fill down at the local bar and cheat on his wife. Everybody in town knew. Everyone except his wife that is. Nobody had the heart to tell her. Some believed that she knew, but that she put up a front to pretend that she had the perfect marriage, but the townspeople all knew better.

Jones passed a few people who said that Robby must have threatened to tell David Cunningham's wife about her husband's affair, and that he had killed Robby in a drunken stupor in order to maintain his silence.

These rumors would eventually be brought to the police, who would look into the man. He would be cleared, as the local bartender had seen the man passed out drunk in his favorite booth during the time when Robby had been murdered.

None of them had any way of knowing that the Briarwood killer was walking amongst them, listening to their fears being announced out loud.

Jones's confidence grew as he realized that nobody expected that it was him. His father grabbed his shoulder and pulled him along as they moved towards the family car.

Several days went by without further incidents in the town of Briarwood, leading the people to relax somewhat and let down their guards. They locked their doors for a few days, but after nothing else had happened, they went back to their normal lives. The mayor still fought to find his son's killer, but time just wasn't on his side. There weren't any cameras around to help solve the murder of Robby Fletcher, and without witnesses, the police had virtually no leads to go on.

The mayor had put out a ten thousand dollar reward for any information that led to the arrest of his son's killer, which was a substantial sum. However, the amount was so high that it only managed to attract those who would do anything for the cash.

The police tip line received numerous phone calls from people who suspected that their friend or neighbor was the killer, but every call turned out to be a hoax, just people willing to snitch on someone they didn't like in order to advance themselves in life monetarily.

Before Jones knew it, life was back to normal.

He walked down the halls of Briarwood High, which were dotted with posters of Robby Fletcher for prom king, each one adorned with a smiling photo of him.

After he died, no one had the nerve to take down the posters, instead, students who passed them in the hall would draw the tips of their fingers across his face as they walked, a sort of remembrance to their former friend.

Jones turned down the senior hallway and saw Robby's locker, which had become a shrine to his passing, as several people had placed flowers or teddy bears, and the entire front of his locker had been covered with cards from mourning students and faculty members.

Jones sneered at the locker and was just about to walk down another hall when he saw Peggy standing nearby.

He turned down the hall opposite her and peered out at her from behind the wall.

What was she doing?

Peggy placed one hand up to a picture of Robby which had been taped to his locker. Her fingertips graced his cheek, and with her other hand, it appeared that she was wiping a tear from her face.

She still had feelings for him, Jones thought.

He couldn't let this go on.

Jones came out from the corner and walked toward Peggy.

"What are you doing?" Jones asked.

Peggy jumped, wiping the last of the tears from her face before turning to face her boyfriend.

"Uh, nothing. I was just, I just..."

Jones took Peggy's hands in his and squeezed them gently.

"Peggy, you know you can talk to me right?" Jones asked. "If something is bothering you, I'm here for you."

Peggy looked down at the floor.

Jones waited patiently, his anticipation growing. He wanted her to tell him about the affair, to tell him that she had made a mistake and that she would spend the rest of her days trying to prove her love for him.

"I appreciate that, Jones. It's just that things like this," she waved her hand at the memorial at Robby's locker. "Remind me how short and precious life is."

That was not what he was expecting her to say. Surely she felt some guilt about the fact that she had cheated on him with the dead kid.

He pressed on, trying to goad her into a confession.

"Did you know Robby? Was he a friend of yours?" Jones asked, watching her reaction.

Peggy dropped her hands from his, letting them swing lightly by her side.

She walked over to her locker, entering her three-digit combo into the lock. Peggy opened the door and stuck her head inside, looking like she was preparing herself to say something to Jones.

"I have to get going to class or I'm going to be late. Can we talk at the County Fair after graduation? I promise I'll be ready to talk by then, once all of this blows over. Okay?" Peggy asked.

She closed her locker and walked off into the distance, leaving Jones standing in the hallway as the bell rang for class.

Suddenly he didn't feel like going.

That's when he heard the footsteps behind him.

He turned to see Max, Kyle, and Carol coming down the hall toward him.

Max and Kyle were both clad in letterman jackets, as they were both on the school's football team, and Carol was wearing her cheerleader uniform.

The school made it a requirement that on game days, all student-athletes had to wear their team uniforms to class or they wouldn't be allowed to play in the game.

The group walked over to Robby's locker, where Kyle banged his fist above the picture of his old teammate.

"I'm gonna miss you, buddy," Kyle said.

Max and Carol touched his shoulder, letting him know that they were there for him.

"We all miss you man," Max said, pressing the palm of his hand on the locker.

Jones decided that that was his cue to get out of there. This particular group of friends wasn't very friendly toward Jones in the past. He was the poor, loser kid and they belonged to the rich and popular clique. Up until recently, Robby led that group.

With Robby in charge, he was able to keep his friend's torments in check, making sure that nothing they did was bad enough that it would get back to his father.

The other kids didn't happen to have the mayor as their dad, so they wouldn't get in as much trouble should they act out.

Robby was held to a higher standard because of who his father was, so whenever he picked on Jones, he made sure that they did it while they were out of sight of teachers and parents.

Without Robby holding them back, the group felt free to do as they pleased. They all came from rich families, so if they were to get into trouble, they could just have their fathers write the school a check and all would be forgiven.

This was a bad combination for kids like Jones, who fell victim to their violence.

If these kids got a bad grade on a test, or if they did poorly in a game, they would take out their anger on the little guy.

Jones didn't want to know how they would deal with mourning their friend, and he didn't want to stick around to find out.

As he turned to leave, he caught the eye of Max, who was the bigger of the two guys.

"Hey, what are you looking at, bozo?" Max said.

Jones didn't say anything, he just kept on walking down the empty hall, hoping that a teacher or a hall monitor would make their way toward him.

"I'm talking to you," Max yelled. "It's rude to ignore someone when they're talking to you."

Jones only sped up, clutching his books to his chest to keep from dropping them. He was beginning to regret his earlier conversation with Peggy, as he was currently across the school from where his classroom was, and there was a lot of ground to cover before there was a safe place for him.

He began to hear footsteps behind him, heavy ones.

Jones made the mistake of looking over his shoulder, just in time to hear Max yell "Get him!"

The group took off toward him, and Jones started to run.

He sprinted down the hall with the group of bullies hot on his heels.

Jones ran in between a group of students, neither of which looked like they would be willing to help him. Instead, they turned and laughed as he was chased away.

Jones was able to get around a second group of students, much larger than the first, and put them in between him and the friends racing after him. They struggled to move the kids out of the way as Jones lengthened the gap between them.

Jones looked over his shoulder and saw that he appeared to be getting away, however, he needed to hide someplace if he wanted to ditch his attackers.

He turned down another hallway and saw his chance.

Up ahead was the classroom door to Mr. Friedman's Social Studies class.

Jones made a beeline for the door, just as he heard the bullies making their way around the corner.

Jones reached the classroom and tugged on the handle.

It didn't budge.

Jones banged on the glass, willing someone to open the door.

Inside, he could see seats filled with people, and at the sound of his banging, Mr. Friedman turned and walked toward him.

Jones had never been happier to see his teacher's face.

He looked to his left and saw his attackers getting closer.

As his teacher walked nearer, he saw his face take on a disappointed look.

Mr. Friedman reached the door, then pointed at the watch on his wrist.

"You're late, Mr. Jepsen. I don't allow tardiness in my class," the man said, before reaching up and grabbing a set of blinds at the top of the door window.

Jones felt his blood run cold as the blinds fell, blocking his view of the class.

He slammed his palm against the door, then took off again, narrowly avoiding Kyle's grasp as he snatched at Jones's shirt.

Jones burst through a set of double doors, then jumped down a flight of stairs, ending up in the boy's locker room.

The room was filled with rows of lockers, with a wall of showers covering one side of the room. Other than the entrance which he had just come in, there were two other exits, both of which led out onto the gym floor.

Jones didn't think he had enough time to make it to those exits.

Jones heard the other guys follow him in, and he hid behind a row of lockers.

He could hear the boys making their way toward him, slamming some of the lockers as they went, kicking people's belongings out of their way.

For a moment, it got really quiet.

Jones didn't have a good feeling about the lack of noise, and he began to walk slowly down the row of lockers, moving closer to the exits that would lead to the gym.

That's when Max stepped out in front of him, blocking his exit.

Jones backpedaled, falling onto his back as Max peered down at him with a smile on his face.

Max began to walk toward Jones, slowly and deliberately.

Jones started to crawl backward, towards the opening at the other end of the row of lockers, but just then, Kyle appeared at the other end.

Jones was trapped.

Chapter Twenty-One

"Please guys, I don't want any trouble from you," Jones said. "Well you see, that's going to be a problem for us, because we came here to start some trouble with you," Max said with a wicked smile.

Max unbuckled his belt and began to pull it from the straps on his jeans. It made a distinct *thwip* sound as it came loose.

Max took a step closer to Jones, bending his belt in half until he had both ends in his hand.

"Get in the shower," Max said, smiling to his friend.

"Wh-what?" Jones stammered.

"I said get in the shower!" Max yelled, whipping Jones's legs with the belt.

Jones cringed, but did as he was told. He stood up, then awkwardly moved passed Kyle, who refused to get out of the way for him.

Jones walked into the showers, which didn't have any lights turned on. He turned around to see what his captors wanted him to do next.

"Take your clothes off," Max said.

"Come on, man. You can't be serious," Jones said.

Max whacked his belt against the wall, commanding a loud crack as he did so.

Jones cringed at the sound. It reminded him of when his dad would whoop him with the belt. He knew what the consequences of disobeying would be.

Reluctantly, he took his clothes off, revealing his pale, skinny figure.

"Turn the water on," Max said.

Jones relented, turning the water on and setting it to a warm temperature.

"Did I say that was the temperature I wanted?" Max asked.

"No," Jones said, his fear rising as he began to pick up on what the boys wanted to do next.

"Turn it up, all the way," Max said.

"But that's going to burn my skin!" Jones protested.

"Do I look like I give a fuck?" Max said, smiling at Kyle.

When Jones paused, thinking about his next move, he received a smack on the back of his leg from Max.

Jones gasped at the sting of the belt as it graced his leg. He looked down and could already see a welt forming.

He looked up at the boys with anger in his eyes, and could only see laughter in theirs. They were toying with him, like a cat playing with its food.

"I'm not doing that," Jones said through gritted teeth, the pain in his leg beginning to ache.

"The fuck did you just say?" Max said. The smile was gone from his face, and at that moment, Jones realized that he didn't see Kyle anymore.

He looked around, just in time to see Kyle coming at him with his own belt.

Kyle began to whip Jones's naked body repeatedly with the belt, and Max soon joined in.

They beat him to the ground, leaving welts across his arms, legs, and torso.

Jones put his arms over his face to protect it, and that only left his stomach open for attacks, and the boys did just that.

Jones felt like his whole body was on fire, and it took him a moment to realize that the boys had turned the water up.

They backed away slightly, and Jones felt the hot water stinging his fresh welts, literally burning his skin.

He tried to get up, but every time he tried to leave the spray of falling water, the boys would smack him back down into it.

Finally, when Jones thought he could take it no more, the boys relented.

"That's enough, boy," Kyle said.

They turned off the water and pulled him to his feet.

"Now get the hell out of our locker room," Max said. "This space is for athletes only."

Jones hobbled over to where his clothes lay, bending over to pick them up.

"Did I say that you could put your clothes back on?" Max said.

"No," Jones said, looking down at his bare feet, which were red and swollen.

Kyle walked over and grabbed the clothes from his hand, then directed Jones toward one of the exits, which led out onto the gym floor.

Jones looked over his shoulder, trying to see if the boys were serious, but he already knew they were.

Jones walked out of the doors to the locker room, into a tunnel that was surrounded on both sides by bleachers.

There was currently a gym class happening, with a group of boys playing a game of basketball. Some of the female students at Briarwood High were on their lunch breaks, and many of them had come to the gym to watch the boys play.

The gym grew quiet as Jones walked out of the tunnel, stark naked and covered in water.

Jones could feel his face growing redder than the welts on his back.

Just then, his world went white.

Had he passed out?

No.

Jones looked down and saw that he was covered in a white powdery substance.

He looked up and saw Carol at the top of the tunnel, a huge grin on her face.

While the guys were tormenting Jones in the locker room, she had gone to the cafeteria and grabbed a bag of flour from the kitchens.

When he walked out of the tunnel, she had dumped the whole bag on top of him.

Because Jones was covered in water, the flour stuck to his skin like it was glued to his body.

Suddenly, the whole gymnasium erupted with laughter.

Jones turned to go back into the tunnel, but the boys were standing there, with belts in hand and huge grins on their faces, blocking the exit.

He was going to have to walk up the bleachers to leave.

Jones turned and saw that everyone had stopped and were staring at him and laughing, including Peggy.

He couldn't bear to show his face anymore.

And he vowed revenge on his attackers.

Chapter Twenty-Two

Before he knew it, graduation was upon them. The school lined up in full cap and gown as they filed into the auditorium.

The chairs were labeled alphabetically, and Jones found his seat pretty quickly, sitting between Elizabeth James and Stanley Johnson.

Jones looked around the crowd of students, searching for Peggy. He found her about two rows back and to the left.

He tried to get her attention, but it was too loud in the room and there were too many people between them.

Before long, the event had started.

All of the faculty were called upon the stage, where they wore gowns decked out in the colors of their alma maters. The principal made a speech about integrity and the students of Briarwood being the shapers of tomorrow, then stepped back to allow the announcer to begin reading the list of names.

The 1963 class of Briarwood High stood up row by row and began their walk to the stage. Because it was in alphabetical order, Jones was still a few rows back and got to watch many of his classmates before him.

Their names were announced, they walked across the stage, shook hands with the principal, and then stopped for a photograph as they were handed a high school diploma.

Jones sneered as Carol Burton's name was called.

She walked across the stage like she owned the place, accepting her degree and then blowing a kiss to the camera.

The announcer got to the F section, and Jeremy Filmore walked across the stage.

When the moment came for Robby Fletcher's name to be called, a hushed silence fell over the room.

Instead of his son, Mayor Fletcher stood up from where he was seated at the back of the faculty. He was a member of the school board, as well as a guest speaker for the event.

He was dressed in a Briarwood blue and gold gown, even though he had graduated from a different school, and Jones realized that the man was wearing his son's cap and gown.

Clutching a photo of Robby in his hands, he walked toward the stage. The principal, though surprised, understood the significance of this gesture and stepped aside, allowing the mayor to stand before the podium.

With a heavy heart and tears glistening in his eyes, the mayor began his speech. His voice quivered, but his determination to honor his son's memory gave him strength.

"Ladies and gentlemen, students, teachers, and friends," he began, his voice carrying a mixture of pain and resolve. "Today is a day that was meant to be filled with celebration and joy, but life has a way of reminding us that it's unpredictable and often unfair. We're gathered here not only to honor the achievements of these young graduates but also to remember someone who should have been among them.

The mayor took a deep breath, composing himself before continuing. "My son, Robby, had dreams that reached higher than the sky. He had aspirations as big as his heart. His life was a testament to hard work, kindness, and an unyielding determination to overcome any obstacle. He was just days away from walking across this stage, his head held high, ready to step into the next chapter of his life."

Jones scoffed. He knew Robby to be an asshole, someone who would put his own needs before anyone else's. The fact that he was such a good athlete was because of his need to stand out above those around him, including his own teammates. Robby had bullied him for years, and had taken advantage of Jones's girlfriend, and for that, Jones took his life.

Jones was the reason that the mayor was up on that stage making this speech. He smiled at the thought of it.

One of his classmates happened to be looking in his direction as he did so.

Max smacked Kyle in the chest and pointed toward Jones, who appeared to be smiling at the idea of the death of their best friend and teammate while his father cried on stage. They began to whisper into each other's ears, no doubt planning something up to no good, unbeknownst to Jones.

His voice growing stronger, the mayor looked out over the sea of faces before him. "But fate had other plans for my son. He was taken from us too soon, in a way that defies understanding and challenges our faith in the world. We're left with a void that can never truly be filled."

Tears streamed down the mayor's face, but he continued, his voice filled with a mix of grief and pride.

"Today, I stand here to accept this diploma on behalf of Robby. I know that he worked tirelessly to earn it, and I want to ensure that his hard work is acknowledged and celebrated. This piece of paper represents not just his academic achievements, but also his resilience, his dreams, and the potential that was stolen from him.

A collective sense of empathy permeated the room as the mayor's words resonated with those in attendance. His speech was a heartfelt tribute to a life tragically cut short, a life that had touched the hearts of many in the community.

"In the face of darkness, let us remember the light that Robby brought into our lives," the mayor concluded, his voice steady despite the tears. "Let us cherish the memories we shared with him and honor his memory by striving to make the world a better place, just as he had hoped to do himself."

As the mayor stepped away from the podium, the room erupted into a mixture of heartfelt applause and tearful silence. The weight of the moment hung heavy in the air, a testament to the power of a father's love and the enduring impact of a young life lost too soon.

The applause died down, and once again the announcer began to shout names into the microphone.

One of the teachers pointed at Jones's line of students to stand up, and they all made their way down the trail of chairs and into the hallway, where they walked to the door that would bring them onto the side of the stage.

From the hallway, Jones could hear the names in front of him being called over the loudspeaker, followed by rounds of applause. You could tell which students were liked more than the rest by the amount of applause they received when their names were called.

The most popular kids would receive a long round of applause followed by screams and whistles, while the nerdier students would have their names called and would then be able to hear the sound of their own footsteps across the stage.

His line was growing shorter, and there were only a few people ahead of him now.

Jones heard a door slam behind him, and he turned to see Max and Kyle storming down the hall. They had seen him smile when Robby's murder had been brought up, and they were pissed.

Jones didn't know what he should do. Should he run and get away from them? He was supposed to walk across the stage in a few minutes, he couldn't miss that.

He took too long to figure out what to do, and in the blink of an eye, they were upon him.

The boys pulled him into a nearby bathroom and shut the door behind them.

Max kept watch at the door, and Kyle tore Jones's gown off of him, then forced him to strip down to his birthday suit. Then Kyle pulled out a marker and began to write on Jones's back. He tried to stop him, but that only resulted in him getting a slap to the face.

Kyle took his clothes and threw them into the toilet, before tossing the gown back to Jones.

"Put it on," Kyle said before he and Max ran out of the room.

Jones stared into the mirror, angry at himself for letting this happen. He slapped the mirror repeatedly with the palm of his hand, not managing to do any damage as it was made with a polished slab of steel rather than glass.

He looked at his clothes in the toilet and knew they were no longer an option, so he put his gown back on, thankful for the ability to walk out of there with something over himself.

Jones opened the bathroom door, just in time to hear his name called on the stage.

He ran over to the opening in the hallway which led to the stairs on the side of the stage, and he made his way into the light.

From his elevated station, he could briefly see his parents in the crowd.

He took one step onto the stage and shook hands with one of his teachers. What he didn't see was Carol standing in the wings behind him.

As Jones began his walk over to accept his degree, Carol poked her leg out and stomped on the back of his oversized gown, piercing it with the heel of her shoe and impaling it to the old wooden floorboards.

Jones didn't realize anything had happened until he heard the ripping sound of the gown tearing itself apart.

The gown was made of cheap material, only meant to be used once. After Kyle had torn it off him and then his body playing tug of war with it against Carol's shoe, the cheap fabric had given out at the zipper line, and Jones had walked right out of it.

He then fell forward onto the stage, stark naked.

All the lights were on him, and every set of eyes in the room as well.

Every student, neighbor, teacher and even his parents were all staring at him in his birthday suit. That would have been bad enough, but then Kyle had written the word "FAGGOT" in giant capital letters across his back, along with a few crude drawings of penises erupting all over him.

He looked up at his principal, who just shook his head at the boy.

Jones looked back at Carol, to show everyone that it wasn't his fault, that this wasn't intentional, but she wasn't there.

Jones's eyes swept the crowd, and he saw her take a seat in the front row, a smile plastered across her face as she enjoyed the show.

He caught movement out of the corner of his eye, and he looked up to see his parents walking out of the room.

Chapter Twenty-Three

Jones's stomach was filled with dread and despair the whole way home from graduation. While he had been embarrassed in front of the whole school, his family, and seemingly the entire town of Briarwood, nothing seemed worse to him than the wrath he would experience at the hands of his father.

His parents had walked out of graduation after Jones had embarrassed himself on the stage, and Jones saw the hate and disappointment in his father's eyes as he left.

They took the car home, so Jones had to walk all the way back to his house wearing nothing but his graduation gown.

He had been publicly embarrassed in front of everyone in the town, and he felt like he couldn't show his face in Briarwood again. As he looked around the crowd, seeing all of the faces laughing at him, he knew that there was no turning back now. There was no saving his reputation, and he couldn't live with people knowing what had happened to him. He knew that every time someone saw him at the grocery store, the first thing they would see in their minds was him falling flat on his face, naked as the day he was born. Nobody would ever take him seriously again.

Jones would kill everyone in that room if he could, starting with Max, Kyle, and Carol.

But all of that would have to wait until he dealt with the wrath of his father.

Jones turned down his driveway, sweat dripping off his forehead and soaking his gown. The oversized garment wasn't really meant to walk in for long distances, especially not in the summer heat. He could feel it sticking to his back as he moved, and one look down would tell him that the pit areas of the gown were soaked through with sweat. To make matters worse, he had to hold the thing shut like a robe or risk flashing the whole neighborhood as he walked.

Jones stopped outside of his house, noting how quiet it was. Normally he would have heard the screams of his father from a mile away, but a look at the driveway told him that his father hadn't come home.

Jones walked inside, seeing his mother at the kitchen table, looking down and ashing a cigarette.

"Ma, I'm so sorry about what happened. I never meant for that to happen," Jones said.

His mother never looked up at him, she just took another long pull of her cigarette.

Jones reckoned that it would be a while before he could get through to her, and he desperately needed to change into a different set of clothes.

He walked into his bedroom, closing the door behind him and locking it.

The day was getting late, and the sun was disappearing behind the fence, casting long shadows through his window.

Jones had barely finished changing into a different outfit when there came a loud bang from the living room.

Jones turned toward his bedroom door, his fear causing goose-bumps to rise up on his arms.

"WHERE IS HE?" his father shouted from the other room. "WHERE IS THE BOY?"

Jones felt himself backing up toward the window, but it was too late to escape.

His father grabbed the handle, giving it a good shake, and Jones was relieved, remembering that he had locked it when he had come into the room.

His father began to pound on the door.

"OPEN THIS DOOR, BOY!" he shouted.

There were several things that Jones was sure of in this world, one of them being that he was never going to open that door. Not while his father was like this.

"I SAID OPEN THE GODDAM DOOR!" his father said, pounding on the door even harder as his anger escalated.

Jones was facing the bedroom door, but his hands were behind him, frantically searching for the window lock. He turned to see what he was doing, when a loud cracking sound came from the entrance to his room.

Jones turned back to the door in time to see the cheap, hollow wood begin to splinter. Pieces of the wood fell down around the floor as his father hit it repeatedly.

There was another loud bang, and his father's fist went through the crack in the wood.

Jones could already see blood dripping from the man's knuckles.

His father was clearly too drunk to feel anything.

He pulled his fist back through the hole, cutting his wrist on the jagged splinters as he did so.

He put his face up against the hole, checking to see if Jones was still there. What he saw angered him even more.

"You're just going to cower there in the corner like a pussy?" his father screamed. "Be a fucking man and open the fucking door!"

Jones felt frozen in place as he watched his father's psychotic rampage unfold in front of him.

Seeing that Jones wasn't opening the door, his father went back to work on it, yanking at the wood around the hole, creating a larger gap.

Jones didn't know how much more abuse the wood could take before it snapped in half altogether.

Finally, the gap was big enough that his father could stick his arm through, and he did just that, reaching inside and grasping for the handle.

Jones snapped to attention, realizing that he was about to be murdered in his childhood bedroom if he didn't do anything.

He ran to his closet, pulling out a wooden Louisville Slugger.

His father's arm was slapping the door as he reached around blindly for the handle.

Jones didn't give him the chance to get to it.

He swung the bat at his father's arm, connecting with a sickening crunch, and he saw the arm bend at a new joint between the elbow and the wrist that hadn't been there before.

His father screamed in pain, then tried to pull his arm back through the hole, yelling out again once he got to the part of his arm that was broken.

Jones heard his father cursing and moving away from the door, and he hoped that his dad's rampage was over, but he couldn't be more wrong.

He had only angered his drunk father even more.

Suddenly, his father's body slammed into the door, and the remaining piece of cheap wood snapped in half as it buckled under his weight.

The man crashed to the ground, landing on his bad arm, the pain only driving his adrenaline-fueled hate rampage even further.

The alcohol in his bloodstream hid his true level of pain from him, and his father jumped up from the ground in a way he hadn't done since his days in the army.

Jones was still stunned at the scene unfolding in front of him, frozen in place, when his father stormed over to him and ripped the bat from his hands.

The man then swung the bat at Jones, who ducked just in time to avoid being hit, dropping onto his stomach on the ground.

His father had swung too hard, and the momentum of the swing, combined with being off balance from the liquor inside him, sent him spinning around like a top.

He corrected himself as Jones was getting up, and brought the end of the bat down upon his son's back, so hard that it snapped in half, creating two jagged ends.

Jones hit the ground once more, this time being slammed there with a bat. He felt the wind get knocked out of him, and he lay there unable to catch his breath. There was a screaming pain coming from his back, and he was grateful that he was still able to feel anything, meaning that his spine hadn't been snapped.

His father looked at the remainder of the bat's handle in his hand, then tossed it away.

For a moment, it looked like he was done, as he began walking toward the door. Jones thought that his father had decided to show him some mercy, but it just wasn't in his nature.

The man swung back around, closing the distance between them, and delivered a swift kick to Jones's ribs.

Jones felt an immense pressure as one of his ribs cracked from the force of the oncoming blow. Unable to stop himself, his body tumbled over, and Jones landed on his aching back, this time caressing his broken ribs.

His father came at him again, raising his foot to stomp on Jones's face.

This man is really trying to kill me, Jones thought to himself.

He needed to react fast, or he would soon catch the business end of his father's size 12 boot to the face.

Jones used what energy he had left to roll back onto his stomach, wincing at the pain in his side.

His father stomped down on the floor hard, and missing his mark threw him off balance once more.

While his father was righting himself, Jones picked up the thick end of the bat which had been broken over his back just moments ago.

One end of it had been turned into a stake, its shaft sharp and full of splinters.

When his father came back to hit him again, Jones was ready.

The man lumbered toward Jones, who was slowly getting to his feet, holding the shaft of the bat behind his back.

Just when the man was about to crash into him, Jones shoved the sharp end of the bat in the direction of his father.

It felt like time had crawled to a stop for Jones, who relished in every moment that came next.

His father had put all his weight forward in an attempt to tackle Jones, and in doing so he was unable to shift his body in time to avoid the bat. His momentum carried him onto it, and there was a sickening squelch as it pierced his chest and sunk itself in his flesh.

The man collapsed onto Jones, who stood firm, supporting the weight of them both. His father's face brushed up against his son's, and he looked into Jones's eyes with a look that said "How could you."

Jones felt his father's blood drip down the piece of wood onto his hand, and it only fueled him to drive the bat further in. The warmth of the blood as it traveled down his arm filled him with adrenaline and made him forget all about the pain he was feeling.

"Am I still a disappointment?" Jones whispered into his father's ear, a smile spreading across his lips.

Jones brought his arms around his father, hugging him for what felt like the first time in his life. He pulled the man close to him, driving the bat even further in.

He saw the pain in his father's eyes, as they rolled back into his head, forgetting where he was.

Jones twisted the bat, before yanking it from its flesh sheath.

It left a baseball-sized hole in his father's chest, and from it poured a waterfall of blood.

Jones dropped the bat to the ground, then watched as the blood drained from the man's face. It grew deathly white, and the man looked back at Jones for the last time. It looked like he was going to say something, but then his eyes glazed over as he succumbed to his injuries.

Jones felt a rush from this experience that he hadn't felt in a while, not since he took the life of Robby Fletcher.

And he felt the need to do it again.

Chapter Twenty-Four

The next evening, Jones took Peggy to the local fairgrounds. The 36th annual Briarwood County Fair was in town, and every year the town would pull all the stops to try to create a fun and enjoyable experience for all of the festival-goers. This year they were trying a little harder, trying to eliminate the fear surrounding the town as a murderer was on the loose.

For all that everyone knew, the murderer could be walking amongst the booths, side by side with them without them even knowing. The idea was to create a distraction from being afraid, enough so that people would drop what they were doing and have fun, and continue to buy tickets to rides and games.

The County Fair was of course a money-making venture overall. Why make fun free when you could monetize it?

Like everything else in the town of Briarwood, when it came to big money-making ventures, there was one man behind it all.

Mr. Fletcher was a big investor in the County Fair, and one would frequently see him roaming the booths, encouraging people to give it another go after they missed the stack of milk bottles with the softball, which would sequentially lead them to spend money on another game.

The way that Mr. Fletcher was carrying about, you would have never known that his son was murdered only a few short days ago.

Jones strolled down the pathway with Peggy, their faces lit up by the flashing lights from all the booths.

Peggy was wowed by the amount of lightbulbs that the festival used and noted that whichever sucker had gotten roped into having the job of changing them whenever they went out had his work cut out for him.

Jones on the other hand was fascinated by all the smells that the fair provided. His nose raised to the air, he inhaled the smell of cotton candy and fried dough. He was salivating at the mouth for these smells that he only got the chance to smell once a year. It made his mother's cooking smell like cow feces in comparison, as his family never had the money to splurge on ingredients that smelled this good.

Jones squeezed Peggy's hand as they walked, enjoying the time he had left with her before he shipped out for basic training. He had decided to forgive her for what she had done to him, mostly because he had gotten the ultimate revenge. In the coliseum of life, he had come out as the victor over his opponent, Robby Fletcher. He had defeated Robby and taken his life for the sins he had committed against him.

His girlfriend's lover was no more, and now she had no reason not to be with him. There was no longer anything stopping her from being with him forever.

Jones placed Peggy's hand to his lips and gave the back of it a kiss. He closed his eyes as he did so, so he didn't note the face she made as he did it.

Peggy pulled her hand away from him, not seeming to know what to do with them, she stuck her hands into her pockets.

"Listen, we need to talk," Peggy said.

She looked around, noting the amount of people around them,

and motioned for him to join her between two tents where they could have some privacy.

Jones smiled, thinking that Peggy wanted to participate in some extracurricular activities with him out of sight of the public eye. He didn't think that she was that kind of girl, but then he thought back to what he had seen in her room the other night and he realized that he didn't know what kind of girl she really was.

Peggy stopped, looking around to make sure that nobody was listening in, then she turned to face Jones.

He smiled up at her, waiting for her to announce her love for him now that he was her only choice. Nothing could have prepared him for what happened next.

"Listen, I know that things have been hard lately for you, what with your family and all," Peggy began. "And I know that you joined the army in an attempt to get away from them and start a career to support us, but I... I don't think I can be in this relationship any longer."

Jones felt like a knife had just been plunged into his heart. He couldn't believe what he was hearing.

Outside the walls of tents that were shielding them from the outside world, the sound of a mallet could be heard slamming against a platform as someone played the high striker game.

Jones flinched as a loud thwack sound echoed its way between the tents to them.

"I don't understand," Jones said. "I thought you loved me. I thought you wanted to spend forever with me."

"I did. But then I got to thinking. I thought about how it would feel to be stuck in this town all alone for years at a time without knowing if you are okay or if you are lying in a ditch somewhere overseas, never knowing if you are going to come home or not. The anxiety of not knowing is stressing me out and you haven't even left yet. I...I think we need to see other people."

Another loud thwack came from the high striker game, making Jones flinch again as the sound reached his ears.

Don't the people playing that game know that people are trying to have a conversation here? Have they no decency?

Jones could feel his blood boiling as he tried to think of a rational thought, of a way to get Peggy to stay with him, but his anger was reaching a tipping point he didn't know if he could come back from.

"See... other... people...?" Jones said between gritted teeth.

As his eyes bared down onto Peggy's, she looked down to hide her gaze from his.

"Who are you going to see? Robby?" Jones spat at Peggy.

She looked up suddenly as if she had been struck.

"Yes, I know all about your little fling with Robby. You didn't think that I was good enough for you. You didn't think that I would be able to provide for you, so you decided to sneak around with the mayor's son. You probably planned to leave me for him this whole time. You were always going to break up with me to be with Robby," Jones said, a vein in his temple growing to the size of a tree root.

"No... No, that's not true..." Peggy stammered out.

"Don't fucking lie to me, Peggy. I went to your house the other night. I was coming over to see you, to run away with you, and leave this town behind. It was my time of need and the only person I could think of was you. So I went to your house, and you know what I saw?" Jones asked.

Peggy could feel her mouth open, but no words came out. She knew what he saw.

"I saw you! With fucking Robby Fletcher! I watched him put his fucking hands all over you. I watched you giggle like a schoolgirl as he undressed you and had his way with you. I thought you were saving yourself for me, but no, the golden boy gets whatever he wants. Including you."

The veins in Jones's forehead were now pulsating. If they got any bigger they would grow legs and walk away. His eyes were crazy, like nothing that Peggy had ever seen before.

There was still something bothering her, besides how this conversation was going.

"That night was the last night I saw Robby," Peggy said. "That was the night that he…"

"Died?" Jones said in a mocking tone. "Yes, if you're asking, I killed Robby. I bashed his fucking brains in."

Peggy threw her hand to her mouth. Tears began to well up in her eyes as she sobbed quietly into her hands.

Another thwack as the mallet hit the platform once more, followed by the ringing of a bell as the person proved their strength by knocking the ball all the way to the top.

"Are you crying for that asshole? I killed him for touching you. I killed him so that we could be together, so that nothing could come between us ever again," Jones said.

"I'm so sorry that you had to do that," Peggy said.

She surprised Jones by throwing her arms around him.

He could feel his anger at her waning as she did this. He felt his arms closing around her, pulling her in tight.

"Thank you for killing Robby. I don't know what I would have done if you hadn't done that," Peggy cried into his chest.

Jones didn't understand what was happening. Was Peggy having a change of heart?

He pulled her in closer.

"Nothing will ever come between us again," Jones said.

A few moments went by, as Jones felt the rest of his anger fade away, then Peggy was the first to pull away.

She wiped her tears with her sleeve.

"If you would excuse me, I need to go find a lady's room to make myself look presentable again," Peggy said.

"Go on, take all the time you need," Jones said, letting go of her.

Peggy made her way to the end of the wall of tents, then looked back at Jones and smiled before walking away.

Jones couldn't believe his luck. He had told Peggy that he had killed her lover and she still wanted to be with him. Things were looking up. They could still be together after all.

Jones walked to the end of the tents, coming back out into the liveliness of the carnival. He took a big sniff, absorbing the smell of cotton candy into his lungs.

Then he looked to his left, seeing Peggy about fifty yards from him, walking at a brisk pace.

As he watched, she turned back to look at him.

Seeing him, she started to run.

Chapter Twenty-Five

Jones's world came crashing down on him. Peggy had played a trick on him. She hadn't forgiven him, she was just trying to get away.

She didn't love him. She was running away to turn him in to the police to bring justice to her lover, Robby.

Jones felt the rage come bursting back to life inside him.

Just then, he heard another loud thwack as someone nearby was playing the high striker game.

He flinched at the noise, which seemed closer now.

Jones looked around and saw a small child hitting the platform with a mallet. However, the child didn't have the strength to reach the bell, so the ball only got as far as the line marked "Weakling" on the pole.

There was an attendant next to the kid. He was holding a stack of bills but wasn't paying attention to the game. He knew the kid wasn't going to hit the bell, it wasn't even worth watching. Instead, the greasy game attendant seemed to be checking out a housewife over at the balloon-popping game.

She was a tall blonde woman, who at the moment was bent over a stroller, trying to console her baby who was scared of the noises coming from the popping balloons.

Jones walked briskly over to the high striker game, not wanting to garner any unwanted attention. Making sure that he wasn't being watched, he picked up a second mallet that was lying near the machine. This one was slightly bigger than the one the child was holding and was meant for adults.

Spinning the mallet over, he marveled at how the weight felt in his hands.

Then he turned and began to jog off with it in Peggy's direction.

The game attendant was still too preoccupied with the woman to notice that anything had happened.

Peggy was much shorter than Jones was, and her small legs were not enough to keep Jones from catching up with her. One moment she was fifty yards from him, and the next moment she could hear him calling her, getting closer and closer. She turned her head, just briefly enough to see Jones closing in on her, this time he was carrying a long wooden mallet.

She needed to get away, and fast.

Peggy put on a burst of energy and ran inside of a nearby attraction. She could hear the attendant outside protesting that she hadn't given him her ticket, but she wasn't stopping. Robby had been a lot bigger than the ride attendant was, so she didn't think he would be able to offer her much protection from Jones.

She needed to get as far away from him as possible.

Jones stopped in front of the attraction to catch his breath. He looked up at it and smiled. This was going to be fun.

"People just don't have any respect these days," muttered the attendant as Jones approached. "Some girl just ran into the mirror maze without giving me her ticket, can you believe that?"

"Here, allow me to pay for her share," Jones said, ripping off two tickets. One for Peggy, and one for himself.

Jones smiled, then walked into the maze.

His boots echoed through the maze as his heels bounced off the metal floor below.

He walked along the path, tracing his hand along the glass so as to make sure he didn't walk into anything. He saw his figure in the mirror, and couldn't help but notice how menacing he looked while holding the mallet over his shoulder.

Jones thought it made him look powerful, a force to be reckoned with.

He didn't mind it.

He had worn the mayor's trench coat and top hat to the fairgrounds. It felt like the type of occasion where dressing up could be fun. He tipped the hat at his reflection and smiled.

Jones stopped checking himself out when he heard a sob coming from somewhere down the path.

He took a few steps, listening as he went. It was hard to distinguish sounds in the maze, as the sound of the festival outside drifted in and drowned out most of the noise from inside.

Jones took a breath, relaxing himself so that he could focus.

Just then, he heard a whimper to his left.

He turned down the path in that direction and then he saw her.

There was Peggy, eyes wide and crying with her hand over her mouth. Her head twisted from side to side as she looked from mirror to mirror to see if Jones was there.

Jones began to walk briskly, picking up speed as he went. He was about five feet from her when he walked face-first into a mirror, bouncing off the glass.

The sound of his face thumping against the glass alerted Peggy, and she looked up, seeing his reflection in the mirrors. She got up from where she was crouched on the floor and began to run, trying her best to navigate the maze as she did so.

"Oh Peggy, come out, come out wherever you are," Jones sang into the maze.

Jones saw Peggy getting away from him and his anger grew. He began to move in her direction once more when he bounced off another pane of glass.

He was going to have to try something else.

Seeing Peggy in a mirror to his right, Jones swung out as hard as he could with the mallet, shattering the glass into a million pieces.

The glass fell in a heap at the base of his feet, pieces falling like snow to the ground.

Jones saw Peggy again, this time in front of him.

He began to walk toward her, glass crunching under his feet.

When he thought he was right upon her he swung the mallet again, this time connecting with the glass once more.

The mirror broke apart, creating a thousand Jones Jepsens as they fell.

Peggy screamed in fear, calling out for help as Jones moved forward on his murderous rampage.

Outside, the attendant took a bite out of the fried dough he had purchased on his break. He was used to people screaming at the fair. He found that most people who tended to make a big fuss would eventually find their way out. He wasn't going to worry himself about going in and getting everyone who thought that they were trapped.

He took another bite of his fried dough.

This stuff gets better every year, he thought to himself.

Inside the maze, Jones was getting closer to Peggy.

The closer he got, the more frustrated she got, and the more often she found herself running into glass.

The amount of times that she had run into dead ends she couldn't count, and it didn't help that every turn looked the same, like her terrified for her life.

"I thought you loved me!" Jones shouted.

"I don't love you, you're a monster!" she yelled back.

Peggy turned a corner and stopped in her tracks.

In the mirror, she could Jones standing behind her.

Peggy ducked as Jones swung the mallet, sending it soaring into the mirror she had just been staring at.

She covered her head as the glass rained down upon her, then she ran with renewed vigor.

Jones was hot on her heels, swinging the mallet wildly behind her, sending glass in her direction with every step he took.

Peggy's lungs began to burn as she felt herself begin to give up. Her hair was filled with shards of glass and the backs of her arms were covered in cuts and scrapes.

Just when she thought that she would never get out of there, she saw daylight. Peggy looked up and saw the exit in front of her.

Using the last of her energy, she burst forward, sprinting toward the exit.

A smile graced her lips as she realized she was going to get out of there.

That's when her forehead bounced off the glass, sending her flying backward to the ground.

She had run into a mirror once again, and this time, Jones was right behind her.

Jones swung his mallet in a downward arc, landing next to her head, but missing intentionally.

Peggy covered her face and rolled to the side, away from the direction the mallet had landed.

"You think that you could just leave me?" Jones said, bringing the mallet down on the other side of her, making a loud clang as it hit the steel floor.

"After all that I've done for you?" Jones swung at the mirror in front of her, sending glass shards down upon her, several of which pierced the skin.

Peggy screamed as a particularly large piece of glass embedded itself in her leg. In doing so, she took her hands off her face to try to remove the glass, which was too painful to move.

As she opened her eyes, she saw Jones had bent down and placed his face only inches from her own.

His face had taken on a demonic characteristic, with eyes that had turned bright red and veins that pulsed in his forehead. His skin had turned blue with the amount of rage that had built up within him.

Gone was the sweet boy who she had dated.

This was a side of Jones that she didn't recognize, that she didn't know could have existed inside him.

"Please Jones, I promise that I can do better. I won't tell anyone that you killed Robby. I'm sorry that I hurt you," Peggy said.

"It's a little too late for that, don't you think?" Jones said, spinning the mallet around in his hands. "You already fucked him. You betrayed my trust, and then you had the nerve to leave me? Well, if I can't have you, no one can."

With that, Jones brought the mallet down upon her, lining up his strike with the tip of the glass shard in her leg.

There was a sickening crunch that echoed throughout the maze, as part of the glass shattered, while the rest drove deeper into her calf and sliced the bottom part of her leg right off.

Peggy looked down in shock, then screamed.

Outside, the attendant just shook his head. He figured that the two were a couple and that the guy who he had let in was chasing his girlfriend through the maze. It was something he had seen time and time again.

"You're next," he said to a girl in line, bending down to retrieve a ticket from her outstretched hand.

Inside the maze, Peggy felt like she was going to pass out from shock. Her right leg was gone below the knee. The lack of blood flow to her head was making her question what her next decision should be. She had to get out of there, away from Jones, but how? Should she try to crawl away? Should she pick up her leg to see if someone could reattach it?

As she stared at the part of her leg that she had grown quite fond of being attached to, Jones kicked it down the hall, sending it flying into a mirror.

There now appeared to be two severed legs over there.

Peggy snapped back into reality, trying to escape from her

deranged boyfriend. She turned onto her stomach, crawling on all four...well, three and a half's, to try to get away. She thought that she was making good progress when she felt Jones plant his foot onto her back.

Jones bent down, grabbing Peggy by the hair and pulling it back hard enough that her back bent into the upward-facing dog position, forcing her to look back at him one last time.

Then he swung the mallet with his free hand, the hammer end connecting with her skull and sending her face in the other direction at a speed that instantly snapped the bones where her brain stem connected to her spine. Her screams instantly died out, replaced with a loud cracking noise.

Jones remarked to himself how much snapping a neck sounded like cracking knuckles.

He threw his girlfriend's useless face to the floor, then used the remainder of his anger to beat her body senseless with the end of the mallet, taking out all of his rage toward her and Robby. He brought the mallet down upon her again and again, enjoying the sight of his handiwork being amplified around him thousands of times in the mirrors. With every swing, Peggy's blood splattered against the glass, until all he could see when he looked around was red.

Outside, the attendant heard a constant banging noise coming from inside the maze.

Exasperated, he climbed out of his booth, pulling the little girl from the door. From the sound of it, the young couple who had walked into the maze a few minutes ago were having sex away from prying eyes. It wasn't the first time this had happened in the maze, but it wasn't the type of thing he would allow to continue happening.

"Hey!" the man shouted. "I need you both to exit the maze immediately!"

As he traversed the maze, he began to see broken glass littering the floor. These guys were going to have to pay for all of the damage they had done to his property, he thought to himself.

He continued, but the banging didn't stop.

"You all are going to pay for what you've done to my maze!" he shouted.

Then he saw something that made his blood run cold.

The glass in front of him was covered in a thick red substance.

He began to back away but only succeeded in backing himself into a corner. He had gotten turned around in there, the blood making him forget his sense of direction.

The attendant took a few steps forward, trying to figure out where he was, when he tripped over something, sending him sprawling to the ground.

His head hit the steel floor below with a bang, one that made him wish that he hadn't gotten up that morning.

As he picked himself up from the floor, he looked back to see what he had tripped over.

It was a human leg.

The man screamed, getting to his feet faster than he had done in the last twenty years, and his body would make him pay for it.

The blood rushed to his head and his vision grew dark. The man stumbled around, trying not to pass out. He placed his hand against one of the mirrors to steady himself, the surface feeling wet to his touch.

As his vision finally cleared, he realized that the mirror he was touching was coated in blood. He brought his hand back in an instant, leaving a giant handprint on the glass.

As he looked into the handprint, he noticed a figure in the background. The mirrors were too coated in blood to get a description of his face, but he could make out a figure dressed in a trench coat and carrying a mallet. He spun around to see, but the glass was too covered in blood to see anything.

It was just then that he realized that the banging sound had stopped.

His blood ran cold as he realized that he was next.

Chapter Twenty-Six

Jones managed to escape the mirror maze, and it wasn't long before the cops arrived and got a description of him from the terrified attendant.

The cops were now on the lookout for a tall white man in a trench coat wearing a top hat and carrying a wooden mallet.

The County Fair was shut down early, as crowds had begun to gather around the mirror maze. Bright yellow police tape was stretched across the entrances to the maze as the police blocked everything off for the gathering of evidence.

The crowds grew larger as time passed, with the police trying to escort people away unsuccessfully. Children clung to their parent's legs as the people of Briarwood waited to see who the newest victim was.

Was it a relative of theirs? A friend? A coworker?

They needed to know, and they weren't going anywhere until they got their answer.

Finally, the coroner arrived on the scene.

As he made his way through the crowd, he stopped to acknowledge several people in the town that he knew. He shook hands with the chief of police, who then pointed him in the direction of the body. The coroner took the steps slowly, not exactly sure what he was walking into.

As the county coroner, his job had been pretty easy. Because murder typically didn't happen in a place like Briarwood, most days he would show up to work, kick his feet up on the desk, and take a nap. Occasionally someone would die and the family would want to know the cause of death in order to know genetically what they had to look forward to. If grandpa died younger than normal due to a heart defect, it may stand that the rest of his family should also get their hearts checked out.

Murder was something that the coroner had never had to deal with. Sure, he had studied cases in college, but he had never had to work a single murder case since taking the job.

As he walked slowly toward the maze entrance, he felt the eyes of everyone in town on him, and he suddenly felt a case of imposter syndrome. Was he the right guy to take care of this? Should he run this up the chain to the coroner in the next county over? Surely there was somebody more experienced who would be able to handle this better than he could.

He reached the top of the steps and turned slowly to face the crowd. These were his neighbors, his friends, and even a few festival attendants who had shut down their rides early and had come to see what the spectacle was about.

He gave them a small wave, then ducked under the police tape and disappeared inside.

A few minutes went by before he was seen again.

The people of Briarwood saw the coroner running out of the maze. His body slammed into the railing at the edge of the stairs as he projectile vomited into the bushes below.

The man puked until the contents of his stomach were depleted, stopping to wipe some of the gunk out of his beard before going back to his car. He returned, this time with a stretcher.

The coroner motioned for a few officers to follow him, who did so reluctantly.

Several moments later, the men returned to the maze entrance. One officer held the tape up while the rest of the men walked into the daylight carrying the stretcher.

The stretcher was occupied, and the body was covered with a white sheet, which was quickly soaking with blood in several places.

As they carried the stretcher down the stairs, Peggy's dismembered leg fell out from under the sheet, bouncing down the steps and coming to a rest at the feet of little Sue Johnson, who was only 8 years old.

The little girl screamed and buried her face into her mother's dress.

One of the officers who was carrying the stretcher had seen the leg falling out and had made an attempt to catch it before it hit the ground.

It was a mistake that would haunt the memories of everyone in attendance for the rest of their lives.

As the man groped for the falling leg, the weight of the stretcher shifted.

The men who were walking down the stairs were unprepared for the change in weight, and the stretcher tilted, sending the corpse of Peggy rolling down the steps.

Her body thudded repeatedly as her broken arms and legs splayed out and smacked against the steel steps. What blood she had left sprayed and splattered on the onlookers scattered around the scene.

Peggy was dead.

Chapter Twenty-Seven

It didn't take long for the police to make the connection between Peggy and Jones Jepsen.

With Briarwood being a small town, many of the people in the crowd were able to make statements on Peggy's behalf about possible enemies, and Jones's name came up a lot. Many people marveled at the fact that Jones was able to land a gal as beautiful as Peggy in the first place, as they had always seen him as the weird kid who tended to stick to himself more often than not.

When bad things happen, people tend to blame the strangest person that they know, and in this case, they happened to be right.

After going to Peggy's house and breaking the news of their daughter's death to her parents, the police received a similar testimony from them. They had never felt that Jones was right for their daughter, as they had always found him to be stranger than most boys his age. They told police that Peggy had told them she was planning on breaking up with Jones, and that they suspected that that may have been the motive for him to end her life.

The police then felt that they had all the motive they needed to go after Jones for questioning.

Jones 1963

That night, the police caused an even bigger scene than there was at the County Fair. Every cop in town was ordered to be on standby to bring Jones in. All of the cops who would normally be patrolling the streets looking for the killer were sent to Jones's house. They felt that if he had killed Peggy, then there was reason to believe that he may have killed Robby as well. If Jones was on a killing spree, then the police wanted as much backup as possible.

The Briarwood police lined their cars up and down the street until they were ready, and then every cop in town converged on the Jepsen house.

Neighbors peered out of their windows as the streets lit up red and blue and sirens pierced the air. Dogs barked and howled at the commotion, only adding to the amount of noise coming from Bleeker Street.

The police ran up to the front door of the Jepsen house, each one decked out in full riot gear.

The police chief motioned for a second team of officers to go around the back of the house, in case Jones tried to escape out of the back door.

A designated officer hammered on the door with his fist.

"Briarwood police department, open up!" the officer shouted.

After nobody answered the door, he banged on it even louder.

"BRIARWOOD POLICE DEPARTMENT, OPEN UP!" the officer yelled once more.

Hearing nothing, he nodded to a special team of officers behind him who were trained to break doors down. The new group of offi-cers walked up to the front door with a pry bar and a ram. The first man stuck the sharp end of the pry bar into the gap between the door frame and the door near where the handle was. Pushing it in as far as he could, he pried the other end of the bar to the left, bending the wood and creating a gap where the latch should be.

The man removed the pry bar and stepped out of the way for a second guy, who carried a ram, which was a heavy metal pipe with two handles on it that was meant to break doors down.

The second officer swung the ram back as much as he could and slammed the end of it into the door, breaking what parts of the locking mechanisms were still attached to the door frame and sending the door swinging open into the wall behind it, where the handle lodged itself into the drywall.

The officer with the ram took several steps back as he was no longer needed. The first team stepped back into place, waiting on the order from their commanding officer.

"Breach, breach, breach," Chief Frank DeSalvo said.

On his command, the group of officers filed into the house, sweeping each room with their weapons as they searched for Jones Jepsen.

"I have something!" one of the officers shouted from the living room.

The rest of the squad came rushing in after clearing the rest of the house. The officer who had shouted was bent down over the motionless body of Jones's mother. One hand was on the hilt of his weapon, while the other was pressed against her throat, feeling for life. She was covered in blood, but the officer was able to detect a faint pulse.

Beside her lay what remained of Mr. Jepsen.

His disfigured body would later be identified by dental records, as there was no part of his body that could be recognized by the naked eye.

The group of police officers observed the scene in horror, spinning around in order to take it all in.

Their guns slowly fell to their sides as their minds tried to comprehend what they were looking at.

Jones had removed his father's hands, then ripped off each finger at the third knuckle. He then used his father's fingers as paintbrushes, with his father's blood as paint. Jones then wrote on the walls in his father's blood, and when one finger dried up, he would discard it for another as if it were a dull crayon.

The walls were covered in words written in the blood of Jones's father.

There didn't seem to be one particular set of handwriting, in fact, it was as if a group of people had written them. Some words were written in all uppercase, and some were written in lowercase, while some were a mix of both. Other times the words grew larger or smaller as they went on.

Written on the walls were names, tons of them. The officers looked around and found the names of their kids, their neighbors, and their friends.

Some names were written larger than others, names such as Max, Kyle, and Carol.

They found Robby Fletcher's name on the wall, already crossed out with a line of dried blood. At the base of the wall lay Jones's father's head. Daniel Jepsen's name was written around his skull, as if Jones had traced an outline of it. It too was crossed out.

Jones had created a hit list.

A list of all the people in town that had made fun of him, laughed at him or didn't come to his aid when he was in trouble.

The list was extensive, and they didn't have enough officers to protect everyone on it.

As the team of police looked around the room, it was pretty clear to them that Jones Jepsen was definitely the Briarwood killer.

And he was going to kill again.

Chapter Twenty-Eight

Deep down, Jones knew that the police were after him and that he needed to skip town, but there were some things that he needed to take care of before he did so.

While the police were surrounding his home, he decided to pay a visit to one of his bullies.

He came to a stop outside of a yellow home on the edge of town with an ivy-covered lattice leading up the side of the house.

The living room curtains lit up with irregular flashing, meaning that someone inside had the television on.

His fingers danced along the mailbox, which read 442 Blackburn Lane. He pulled open the door to the box, reaching inside and grabbing the mail.

Jones sifted through the mail until he found the name that he was looking for, then he tossed it over his shoulder before closing the box. He took a deep breath, and then he swung his mallet in an upward arc, connecting with the side of the box and removing it from its post. He watched as the box soared across the lawn, coming to a stop underneath one of the bushes.

A moment later, Carol Burton's face peered out from the curtains as she looked for where the sound originated from. She looked into the darkness but saw nothing out of the ordinary. Even so, a chill ran up her spine.

Carol shut the curtains and decided that she needed to check on her little brother.

She walked up the stairs, carefully stepping around the spots that she knew to be creaky. Carol had no reason to be quiet, but it was a habit that she had picked up after several years of sneaking out of the house.

She knocked on her brother's door and opened it to find him playing with trucks on the ground. The room was decorated with wallpaper that depicted bright red firetrucks. There were a few pieces of furniture in the room, including a bed on either side for when her little brother had friends over.

"Hey buddy," Carol said. "Aren't you supposed to be in bed?"

"I know," Timmy said. "I couldn't sleep."

"Well it's passed your bedtime and Mom and Dad would kill me if they knew that you were still up," Carol said. "Why don't you clean this mess up and try closing your eyes for a bit?"

"Ugh, fine," Timmy said. He began walking around the room, picking up his toys and tossing them into a bin in the corner of the room.

Just then, they heard a loud crash from downstairs.

"What was that?" Timmy asked.

"I don't know, maybe Mom and Dad are home," Carol suggested.

She walked over to the window, but the driveway outside was empty of cars. It wasn't their parents.

Carol began to feel fear rising in her chest, but she knew that she needed to be strong for her brother. If she freaked out, then her brother would freak out, and then he would never go back to sleep.

"Maybe it was the TV, I think I left it on downstairs," Carol said. She began walking toward the door. "Or it could have been a bird crashing into the window, they probably can't see very well at night."

Carol opened the door and walked into the hallway. She couldn't hear anything else, but she still wanted to be cautious.

She turned back to her brother.

"Stay here while I go check it out," Carol said.

"What? No! I want to check out the bird," Timmy protested.

"No, it could be dangerous. Promise me that you'll stay here," Carol said.

"Fine. I promise," Timmy said, folding his arms over his chest.

Carol closed the door behind her and began inching down the steps. She got about halfway down when she saw the pieces of broken glass on the living room floor.

Maybe it actually was a bird, she thought to herself, but dismissed that thought immediately after she took a few more steps.

Her breath caught in her throat as she saw the back of a man standing in her living room. He was dressed in a trench coat and carrying a wooden mallet, the kind that you would see at a carnival game. The man was bent over, staring at the family photos placed on a shelf in the corner.

She had just begun to back slowly up the steps, with her hand clasped firmly over her own mouth when the man grabbed a photo of Carol off the shelf and slammed it onto the ground, sending shards of glass into the carpet.

Carol tried not to scream as the sound echoed across the house.

She had just moved out of sight when the man turned around and spoke for the first time.

"Come out, come out wherever you are," the man said.

Carol recognized that voice.

It belonged to the kid that she had made fun of in school.

It belonged to Jones Jepsen.

Chapter Twenty-Nine

"Briarwood Police Department, what's your emergency?" Helene asked. She was at the end of her shift, with only about twenty minutes left to go before she could hang up her phone and go home. Being an operator at the Briarwood Police Department was an easy job. When she applied for the job four years ago, she had expected that she would be dealing with some horrific phone calls from people on the worst day of their lives, however, that just wasn't the case.

Briarwood was a peaceful town where not many bad things happened. Most of the time when she received a call, it was because someone's cat was stuck in a tree, or somebody's grandmother had fallen in the bathtub and needed some help getting out.

Nothing could have prepared her for the phone call she was about to receive.

"Briarwood Police Department, what's your emergency?" she repeated. Sometimes children got ahold of the phone and liked to press buttons, then drop the phone when the police answered. The police were usually the only number that parents would teach their kids to call in case of an emergency, so this type of thing happened often. Helene thought that this may be the case, and after a few more seconds of silence, she was about to return the phone to the receiver, but then she heard the panic-stricken voice on the other end.

"You've got to help us," a terrified voice sounded in a frantic whisper. "There's somebody in the house. I think he's come to kill us."

Helene's voice caught in her throat. She had never received a call like this, she had almost forgotten the protocol for what to do with a case like this. She would have dismissed it altogether as a prank phone call, but there had been a string of murders in the town of Briarwood recently. Was the person on the other end of the phone about to be the next victim?

"Uh, um." Helene cleared her throat and tried again, resolving that if this call was real, then the girl on the other end needed Helene to be strong for her, to be a resounding voice at a time of confusion.

She tried again.

"You said there's somebody in the house? What is your name and the address you are calling from?" Helene asked.

Silence. Helene feared that she may have already been too late.

"Ma'am, I need an address to send the police to you. May I have the address from which you're calling?" Helene asked.

"My name is Carol and my address is 442 Blackburn Lane," the voice on the other end whispered.

Helene scratched the address onto a sheet of paper in front of her. She would direct the police to that address once she was able to get some more information out of the call. She needed to be able to discern what kind of police presence she needed to send to the house and be able to determine if there was indeed a threat on the premises. She learned in her training that sometimes people called about break-ins only to find out that it was their husband who had come home drunk and forgotten his keys at the bar. Even if that were the case, she was still required to send an officer to do a wellness check all the same.

"You said us, does that mean that there is somebody else in the house with you?" Helene asked, holding her pencil still as she waited for the caller's response.

"My brother," Carol whispered. "I was in charge of babysitting him tonight. We are both hiding under our beds upstairs, please hurry."

Helene marked the girl's response on her sheet of paper. Now that she knew who was supposed to be in the house, she would be able to alert the police to who should not be in the building.

"You said that you are babysitting tonight, where are your parents?" Helene asked.

"They are visiting my aunt in the next state over," Carol whispered.

Helene paused her note-taking.

"Well how do you know that the person in your house isn't your parents?" she asked.

"Because I heard his voice. I know who the intruder is," Carol said quietly into the phone.

"Who is it?" Helene asked.

"It's Jones Jepsen."

Helene shot up, sending her chair flying to the ground as she did so. She placed the phone on the table and ran to the window behind her. Just then, she remembered the sheet of paper, and she doubled back to get it.

Helene ran back to the window, where she called for help from any nearby officers.

She yelled for help once more, and a few seconds later, a chubby officer rounded the corner, a cup of steaming hot coffee still in his hand. He must have come as quick as he could and had sloshed coffee all over the front of his uniform as he ran. He came to a stop in front of her office window, huffing and puffing and trying to wipe some of the fresh coffee from his shirt.

"What's the matter, Helene? Have you seen a mouse?" the man asked, assuming that nothing real could have alerted her to this point.

"I have a caller on the line who says that Jones Jepsen has broken into her house. Here's the address," Helene said, shoving the piece of paper toward him.

At the sound of Jones's name, the officer dropped the cup of coffee to the ground, where it shattered, sending up a wave of coffee and ceramics across the floor.

He ripped the sheet of paper out of her hand, forgetting that he was out of breath as he ran back to the front of the station. With one hand he held the sheet of paper, with the other he reached up to his shoulder and pressed the button on the side of his radio.

"Calling all available units, I have a report of Jones Jepsen in an ongoing home invasion at 442 Blackburn Lane. Please be advised that we have two subjects hiding on the second floor of the residence. Suspect is to be treated as armed and dangerous."

Chapter Thirty

Jones Jepsen swung the end of his mallet back and forth, creating a whooshing sound as he did so. He turned his neck to the left and right until he heard a satisfying crack, feeling like he would need a good stretch, as it would be a very long night.

"Come out, come out, wherever you are," Jones said, turning to get a good look at his surroundings.

He was standing inside the living room of the Burton household, which was much cozier than his own house. Like the Fletcher family, the Burton family had a taste for expensive things. They weren't nearly as wealthy as the Fletchers, but they liked to pretend that they were. They tended to buy all of the latest things the moment they came out. This was actually the first house in town to have a television set.

The Burtons weren't exactly flush with cash, they just liked people to think they were. In reality, the family was money-poor but rich in things. They spent their money the moment they got it and barely had enough left over to get by.

As Jones looked around, he could see the result of their gluttony.

In the living room, there was a massive stone fireplace. Across from it sat a very large avocado-green sofa and two wicker armchairs. The walls were covered in floral wallpaper, dotted here and there with family photos.

Jones bent down to examine one such photo. He could only imagine the time and work it must have taken to get everyone to sit still and pretend they were happy for the amount of time it took to take the picture. He knew that behind every one of their fake smiles was an urge to rip off the scratchy matching sweaters and get the hell out of that photo studio. He spotted the mother in the family, who seemed to be the only one genuinely happy to be there, and he guessed that she was the one who had organized the photo shoot.

He stepped onto a large, white shag carpet, marveling at how much his feet sunk into the furry, textured fabric. Then he wiped the mud off his feet and continued around the house.

The television set was still on, as Carol hadn't shut it off when she had walked up the stairs. An episode of General Hospital was playing, and Jones walked over to the set and swiped his hand in front of the screen, feeling the static brush across his fingertips. He bent down and turned the volume up, he didn't want the neighbors to hear something they shouldn't and get any bright ideas about coming over.

He had been hiding behind the bushes when Carol had opened the curtains, so he knew that she was there. She couldn't hide from him for long.

"Oh Carol, why don't you be a big girl and come out and play? I know you're here," Jones said.

He had made his way into the kitchen and saw a mug of tea on the counter. He picked it up, noting that its contents were still hot.

Jones brought the cup to his lips, taking a sip of the beverage before spitting it out and throwing the mug against the wall, where it smashed and dripped brown water and excess tea leaves down to the floor.

He had never had tea before, but now he couldn't help but wonder how so many people could enjoy that horrible drink.

As the pieces of the mug hit the ground, he thought he heard a noise from upstairs.

Jones smiled a wicked smile, knowing that it wouldn't be long before he got what he wanted.

He walked towards the stairs, spotting a line of family photos on the wall going all the way up the steps.

How many photos can one family take? Jones thought to himself.

Jones crept up the stairs one by one, cringing to himself as he landed on a creaky step. It wasn't like he was trying his best to be quiet, he had announced himself earlier, however, he felt as though it gave away his position, giving Carol an opportunity to move farther away from where she knew he was.

"I know you're up here," Jones said as he crested the top of the stairs.

As he stared down the long, dark hallway, he saw light coming from underneath one door.

He smiled, knowing that he had Carol trapped with nowhere to go.

Jones inched closer to the door, once again cringing as a loud creak came from the floorboards beneath his feet.

For a family who spent so much money on nice things, they should really look into fixing their floors, Jones thought to himself.

Just then, he thought he heard whispering from inside the room. He placed his ear to the door and thought he could make out the sound of whimpering.

He smiled. He liked to think that he was striking fear into the heart of his high school bully, that she was shaking in her boots on the other side of the door. He gave her a few more seconds to be afraid, to wonder what was waiting for her in the hallway, before he grabbed the handle and turned.

A sudden hush fell over the room as the door swung open. Jones was temporarily blinded as he walked into the brightly lit room from the dark hallway.

He spun around with the mallet, looking for Carol, but there was nobody there.

Jones could've sworn that he had heard noises coming from inside the room.

That's when he saw the receiver end of the phone.

He found it strange that a young boy would have his own phone line, but then he remembered that the Burton family was frivolous with their spending.

Jones walked over to the receiver, but the phone was not resting on its cradle.

He followed the phone line with his eyes, and he saw that one end of the line went underneath the bed.

Jones smiled and pressed down on the receiver button, hanging up the phone.

Chapter Thirty-One

Carol had gone deathly quiet as her fear prevented her from breathing. Under the bed to her left, her brother wore an equally scared expression, with his hands covering his mouth to avoid giving himself away.

Carol's hands gripped the phone with such force that her fingers had begun to lose circulation. If she were to squeeze the plastic device any harder, it would definitely give away her position.

The door swung open, and she saw Jones pause at the front door.

She followed his feet with her eyes as he slowly examined the room. At one point, it looked as if he were staring out the window.

That's when the phone line went dead.

Suddenly, the sound of the phone's dial tone went off in her ear.

It was probably not very loud, but in this situation, it was deafening.

Carol turned to the phone, trying to figure out a way to stop the noise.

She fumbled with the phone, before ripping out the phone cord with an audible click.

She had tried to be quiet, but it was too late.

A pair of dirty white hands reached under the bed and grabbed the first thing they could find.

As Carol looked on in horror, Jones Jepsen grasped her little brother by the ankles and pulled him out from under the bed.

His eyes filled with terror as he reached out to his sister to help.

Her brother locked onto her wrists, willing himself the strength to resist the man who wished to kill them.

Jones pulled harder, becoming too much for her brother.

His fingers dug into her wrists as he was pulled away, leaving bright red gouges in her flesh that immediately began to bleed.

She would never forget the look of fear in his eyes as he was dragged across the carpet, the look that begged his sister to help him.

But she was too frozen with fear to do anything.

She could do nothing but cry in silence as she watched the mallet fall down upon his skull.

She felt the impact on his head as if it were her own, mostly because pieces of it splattered against her face under the bed.

Carol was screaming internally but her face was permanently stuck in a state of shock, unable to perceive the fact that her brother was dead.

She would never be able to see him again.

She would never again be able to call him a brat, or hear his voice from the other side of the door yelling at her to hurry up in the bathroom.

Her brother was dead, and she was next.

Jones took one last swing, then picked up her brother's limp body to make sure he was dead.

Satisfied that he did a good job, he dropped her brother's carcass to the ground, where his face turned to look at her one last time.

Carol couldn't help but stare into those lifeless eyes, that looked like they could see her, but also saw right through her.

Just then, a new face replaced her brother's, as Jones Jepsen dropped to the floor.

Carol screamed as Jones's blood-spattered face smiled from ear to ear.

She began to squirm backward to get away from him, and Jones crawled under the bed after her.

There wasn't much room to move around under the bed, and as Jones made his way closer to her, his back pressed the bed up, and it moved as he moved.

Carol screamed again as Jones barked at her, and she scrambled out from under the bed.

She turned to look at her brother's mutilated body, but she very much wished that she hadn't. It no longer looked like the boy that she knew, and that beaten, bloodied image of him would be seared into her brain for as long as she lived.

Carol knew that she needed to get out of this room, to get as far away from Jones as possible, and she turned and began to run toward the door.

Suddenly, she felt a hand grasp her ankle, and her body came crashing down onto the carpet as Jones grabbed her from under the bed.

She screamed once more, this time in anger, and she kicked out at Jones's smiling face under the bed.

Her Converse size 8 shoe connected, drawing blood at the corner of Jones's mouth. With his free hand, he wiped the blood from his mouth, and then smiled back at her, this time with vengeance in his eyes.

He began to pull Carol back under the bed, closer to him.

She reached out for anything she could to prevent her descent under the bed, but there was nothing. She felt the rug burn on her back as her shirt rode up and the friction between her skin and the carpet fibers caused a stinging sensation.

Carol needed to get out of this somehow, and she felt an animalistic urge to survive overtake her. She began to kick out once more, forcing Jones to free up his hands to block her foot from connecting with his face.

Suddenly, he caught her foot in one hand, locking on.

She kicked again, and this time the shoe came off in Jones's hand.

Carol scrambled back to her feet, limping toward the hall wearing only one shoe.

"No!" Jones screamed from under the bed, and Carol could hear the sound of the bed hitting the wall as he stood up rather than bothering to crawl out.

Carol took the stairs two at a time, then raced to the kitchen, where she knew another house phone was attached to the wall.

She had to be quick because Jones would be downstairs in a few moments. She had to call the police again or warn her parents not to come home, or get help from somebody, anybody. She couldn't think straight, she kept thinking of her brother's lifeless body on the floor staring at her.

Carol ran over to the wall and picked the phone off of the receiver, pressing it to her ear as she tried to dial a number. Her mind was so full of panic that she couldn't think of any numbers. Her finger rested in one of the number holes on the rotary phone, and only then did she realize that something was off.

There was no dial tone coming from the other end.

She took a moment to examine the phone and saw that the cord had been cut.

Carol let the phone fall from her face, and it clattered to the ground without the wire to keep it from hitting the floor.

If she couldn't call for help, then she would have to go out and find somebody.

Were her neighbors home? She couldn't remember.

It was hard for her to think, and General Hospital sounded like it was turned up to max volume, but it could just be her nerves overreacting.

She had to get out of the house.

Carol ran over to the sliding glass door in the kitchen, and as she went to unlock it, she saw the reflection of a figure behind her.

She turned to see Jones power walking across the room toward her.

He raised up his mallet to swing but connected with nothing but air as Carol opened the door and burst out into the night, the sound of General Hospital blaring out after her.

Carol ran across the yard, completely out of breath from running through the house.

She tried to scream for help, but the words never came out. Instead, she tasted a mouthful of dirt as Jones threw his mallet, striking her in the back of the head and sending her to the ground.

Carol tried to move, to get up and run, or scream, but her body didn't want to do anything.

With a pang of fear, she realized that she couldn't move a muscle, her body was paralyzed.

All she could do was mumble through the mouthful of leaves and dirt as she saw the outline of Jones Jepsen in the light from the sliding glass doorway.

As he grew closer to her, her muffled screams were drowned out by the sound of the television.

She couldn't help but wonder where any of her neighbors were. Had they seen what happened? Would they come to her rescue?

A single tear fell down her cheek as Jones bent down to be face-to-face with her.

He waited for her to move, to resist in some way, but she couldn't.

Jones smiled, then grabbed her by the hair and began to drag her limp body back inside the house. He wasn't done with her yet.

Chapter Thirty-Two

Lights surrounded the residence of 442 Blackburn Lane. The cops had arrived finally, but it was already too late, Jones was gone.

He had left a mess of bodies in his wake, and the last remaining thing the parents would have of their children was the recording of the 911 call.

Officer Frank DeSalvo had arrived on the scene first, and what he had seen mortified him, so much so that when the rest of the Briarwood police arrived, he had them all take a knee outside for a briefing.

Frank had been close with the Burton family, so it pained him to see the things that were now burnt into his eyelids.

As the last of the police arrived, he gestured for them to gather around him in front of the house.

Frank stood at the top of the porch, staring at the stars to avoid eye contact with his men. He feared that was all it would take to make him break down and cry in front of them.

"Listen up men. This crime scene is like none other that I have seen in my years on the force. Dispatch says that the suspect in the house was Jones Jepsen, and it appears that he is getting increasingly violent in his ways. He is showing a lack of restraint upon those who he kills. Most serial killers stick to a type. It might be brunettes, or people who remind them of a parent. Most of them still have the decency to stay away from children. Jones... well he's not that decent."

Frank took a moment to look back through the glass of the front door. The porch was raised up, so none of his men had been able to see through the windows yet. None of them had seen what he had.

He turned back to his men, wondering how he could word what he needed to say.

"There appears to be two victims tonight. Carol and Percy Burton."

A volley of cries went up from the officers.

"God dammit," one man said, turning away from the group to hide his emotions.

The Burton family was very active in the community, and with it being such a small town, their children had grown up with the officer's own children, had played at their houses, and had sleepovers together.

"The victims were eight and seventeen years old, and their deaths were pretty brutal. Before you enter this house, I would like you to prepare yourself for what you are about to see. This crime scene is very graphic, so if you don't think that you can handle it, I advise that you stay outside and guard the perimeter. As your chief, I don't want to force any of you to see something that you won't be able to unsee, however, I am asking for any volunteers who would be willing to come inside and document the crime scene and collect evidence."

There was a brief pause while each of the men considered the risks at hand. From what their chief was describing, it sounded like it was a warzone, where many of them may see pictures of the dead running through their minds years after the event had ended. The victims were kids, taken far too young, and would remind them of what could happen to their own kids.

Finally, two men stepped forward, while several others moved back to set up the perimeter.

A few other men just stood still. It wasn't clear if they were deciding which route to take, or if they were mourning two people from their neighborhood. The Briarwood police department was a pretty cozy job, as many had never experienced much crime other than the average domestic dispute or the random drunk guy walking the streets.

This was a whole other level that they weren't prepared for. Seeing the dead bodies of their friends and neighbors on a daily basis was making them question whether or not they should stay with the force.

Some of the officers began wrapping the exterior of the house with yellow caution tape, while the two who followed their chief ascended the stairs to the front porch.

The chief paused with his hand on the door handle, and he turned to look the other officers in the eye.

"Are you sure you're ready for this?" Frank asked.

The men didn't answer right away, their gazes didn't meet up with Frank's. Rather, they were looking past him, towards the glass window of the door, where all they could see was red.

"Yeah, we're ready," one officer said, and the other nodded.

The chief nodded back, taking a breath to steady himself, then opened the door.

The once clean and tidy room was now torn apart. Jones had ripped every photo off the walls and shelves, tossing them onto the floor before stomping on them. He then took the broken shards of glass and shoved the sharp ends into the faces of each of the family members in the photos.

The television set was still playing General Hospital, and one of the officers walked over and turned the knob, watching as the light on the screen shrunk into a tiny dot in the middle before disappearing altogether.

Frank was in the kitchen, where he found the sliding glass door open.

He looked up at the ceiling, where it looked like a hundred moths and mosquitoes had come inside and were now attacking the kitchen light.

Frank ducked to avoid the bugs and bent down to look at the trail of blood that traveled through the sliding glass door into the house.

There didn't appear to be any shifts in the drag marks, which would mean that the body being dragged must not have struggled, and that the person was already dead when they were being moved, or so he hoped.

Frank motioned for one of the other officers to photograph the drag marks, and to close the doors to prevent more bugs from getting in and messing with the crime scene.

He followed the bloody trail to the stairs, where it appeared that Jones had dragged the corpse up the steps.

Frank didn't have to follow anymore to realize what Jones did next.

Near the top of the stairs, there was a brief space with a railing that overlooked the hallway below, creating a mini balcony. A thick rope was tied to the railing, and on the other end of the rope was Carol's lifeless body, or what remained of it.

Jones had tied her body up in a harness fashion, with ropes fastened around her shoulders and thighs. He had also managed to hang her with her face pointed towards the ground.

Jones had then come back down the stairs, at which point he had used Carol's body as a pinata, smacking it around with his mallet until all of her insides came out and splattered to the ground.

Frank looked down at the ground near his feet in disgust, careful not to tread in any of Carol's blood, which had become a hard task to accomplish as it was everywhere.

He had forgotten to warn his deputy in the other room, who at that moment walked around the corner with his camera.

The man stopped in his tracks, letting the camera fall loosely to his side, the strap around his neck being the only thing saving it from an untimely demise.

The deputy ran out of the room, and Frank could hear him tossing up his lunch on the lawn outside.

Wait until he sees the kid upstairs, Frank thought to himself.

Just then, he heard the sound of tires screeching as a car pulled into the driveway.

Frank ran outside in time to see Carol's parents burst out of their car. They ran from the vehicle, not stopping long enough to close their car doors all the way.

Frank walked toward them as they fought one of the deputies at the perimeter to get through.

He recognized them and waved to his deputy to let them through.

They ducked under the police tape and made their way toward Frank.

"What happened?" Richard Burton yelled to Frank, even though he was only a few feet in front of him. "Are the kids all right? The house isn't on fire, what are you all doing here?"

"One of the neighbors called and said that the police were at our house, and we drove as fast as we could back home. What's going on?" Debbie Burton asked.

"Um, I don't know the best way to tell you this," Frank began.

"Tell us what? What happened?" Richard asked.

Frank stuttered, trying to find the best way to tell his friends that both of their children were brutally murdered, but he didn't get the chance to.

Richard Burton's eyes looked over Frank's shoulder, to where he had left the front door open, and he saw the walls painted in the blood of his children.

Richard pushed Frank out of the way, and he didn't have the nerve to stop him. He didn't feel like anything he could do at that moment would have any effect on him, that he was going to run into that house whether Frank liked it or not.

Debbie Burton followed her husband as he took the front porch steps two at a time, pausing once he got to the front door.

Frank looked away, toward the houses of the neighbors, most of which were standing outside their homes at this point.

He didn't want to see the look on their faces when they saw that their children were dead, but he heard it, and the sound of their screams would haunt him forever.

When Frank finally walked back inside, he found Debbie sitting at the kitchen table, a blank look in her eyes as she held a fresh mug of coffee. It was one of the few things she did that made her feel normal on a day-to-day basis, and she felt the need to do it now to calm her nerves. She hadn't taken a sip, just held onto the cup, trying to prevent her hands from shaking.

It took Frank and a few officers several minutes to pin down Richard, to prevent him from taking his daughter's corpse down before they could document the rest of the crime scene.

The man was sobbing uncontrollably and calling out his kid's names, blaming himself for not being there when his kids were being murdered.

Finally, all of the evidence had been collected, and the coroner had arrived to collect the bodies.

Frank stood outside with the parents as the funeral home brought two body bags out on stretchers and brought them to the car.

Carol's parents watched as the doors shut, and the vehicle drove away with their dead children.

"I promise that I will try to get this guy before he kills any more kids," Frank said.

Richard turned to Frank, shoving a long, shaky finger into his chest.

"You better catch this son of a bitch before I do," Richard said, between gritted teeth.

Chapter Thirty-Three

"Your daughter made a phone call to the police while all of this was happening," Chief Frank DeSalvo said. "She seemed to believe that the person in the house was Jones Jepsen. While I am inclined to believe her, and I have reason to believe that Jones is responsible for all of the murders happening in Briarwood as of late, I need to make sure that her assessment is true before I charge him with another murder. Had your daughter ever done anything to piss him off?"

"Are you trying to blame my daughter for her own murder, Frank?" Richard asked, his tone growing defensive.

"No, I'm simply trying to figure out what makes Jones tick, what his motives were that drove him to kill all these people, and where he may be headed next," Frank said.

Debbie placed her hands on Richard's, and he calmed down as he turned toward her. She looked him in the eyes and gave him a look that told him that she knew more than she was letting on.

"I heard Carol on the phone the other day. I picked up the phone downstairs and tried to call my sister, Betty, the one down in Collinsville. See, Betty is expecting another child, and I was planning on calling her to see how she felt so that we could expect when we would need to go out there and see the baby. Anyway, I picked up the phone downstairs and before I could begin to dial, I heard Carol on the other end talking to that boy Max. She's good friends with Max and Kyle, we've summered with their families out in the Hamptons. Well, I was fixing to hang up and give her a moment to finish her call, but then I heard them mention that they were planning something. Something awful. They were talking about that Jepsen boy." Debbie's hands went up to her face as she began to cry into them.

Richard placed his hand on her shoulder, trying to soothe her.

"It sounded like they were just going to play a prank on the boy, I didn't think anything like this would happen," Debbie sobbed between her fingers. "If I had just said something to her, and prevented her from doing it, our baby would still be alive right now."

Chief Frank DeSalvo remembered back to the graduation event. He hadn't been there personally, but it was a small town, and word traveled here quickly. Jones had been embarrassed in front of his whole community, and now he was taking action against the individuals who had wronged him.

Suddenly, he knew where Jones was headed next.

Frank was halfway out of the house when he reached for the radio on his shoulder.

"I need all available units to the Henderson residence. I have reason to believe Jones is headed there next!"

And indeed he was.

Jones had just romped through the woods, making his way a few streets down to where Max's house was located. On his way there, he had seen the lights of the police fly by, going back toward the way he had come.

They were going in the wrong direction, and would always be several steps behind him, following around to clean up his mess when he was done. They would be too preoccupied at the Burton house to handle what was coming next, and they wouldn't make it in time to save dear old Max.

Jones made his way out of the grove of trees, brushing a few stray twigs off of his trench coat. He took in a deep breath, hoping for fresh air, but it still smelled of the brick factory even this far away.

He knew the cops wouldn't be too far behind, so he had to make this quick. He couldn't sit and wait for the perfect moment like he had done in the past.

Jones crossed the street, sticking to the shadows so he wouldn't be seen. There weren't any lights on in the house, and he assumed that Max would be sleeping. He couldn't wait to see the look on his face when he woke up and saw Jones standing over him. He wanted Max to be awake when he killed him, to see what he was doing to him. To kill him while he was asleep would be such a waste.

Jones had a hunch, and he walked right up the steps to the front door. He grasped the handle, waiting for a few moments to hear if there was any movement inside. Hearing nothing from the other side, he turned the handle, not surprised to find that the door opened without a sound.

Most people in Briarwood kept their doors unlocked because it had always been a peaceful town. Even after the police warned the town that there was a serial killer on the loose, the Hendersons still thought of themselves as too important to lock their doors. They must not have thought that anyone would have dared trespass on their property.

Jones stepped into the dark house, taking a moment to let his eyes adjust to the light.

The house seemed pretty similar to Carol's home, but Jones wasn't going to take the time to look around. He was there for one thing and one thing only, to take the life of Max Henderson.

He tightened his grip on the mallet, its end still covered in Carol's blood, then made his way toward the stairs.

As Jones walked up the steps, he thought about the things he would do to his bully, and his smile grew wider. He didn't want to make a noise, to alert Max or his family to his presence. Besides, his grudge wasn't with the Henderson family, it was with Max, but he wouldn't hesitate to strike them down if they got in the way.

Finally, he reached Max's door. Jones took a deep breath outside it, centering himself, creating a plan in his mind of what he should do once he got inside.

Then he opened the door.

Chapter Thirty-Four

There was nobody there. Jones checked every part of the room where Max could be, under the bed and in the closet, but he couldn't find his bully anywhere. He did a search of the rest of the rooms in the house, only to turn up nothing.

No members of the Henderson family were home.

Jones was about ready to leave, to chalk this venture up as a waste of time and go on his merry way.

That's when he saw the headlights pull into the driveway.

Jones ran to the window, just in time to see Max get out of the Jaguar his family had given him as a sixteenth birthday present.

Max got out and closed the door behind him, tossing the keys up in the air and catching them.

As Max made his way toward the front door, Jones got an idea that gave him goosebumps.

He tried to imagine Max's face if he were to open the front door and see Jones standing in the doorway waiting for him. A smile spread across his face, and he knew he needed to make it happen.

Jones ran to the front door as quietly as he could.

Once there, he paused in front of it, mallet in front of him, posing in a way where he could jump out and scare the shit out of Max before dragging him inside and making him his bitch.

He could hear Max drawing closer, he was whistling a tune that was popular on the radio at the time, but Jones couldn't remember the name of it. All he could think of was the joy he would get from ending the life of the boy who had given him hell throughout his teenage years.

He heard Max's heavy footsteps on the front porch, the wood creaking under his steps.

Jones's heart was about ready to beat out of his chest when the handle began to turn.

He could see the shadowy outline of Max through the frosted glass at the top of the door. It was too dark inside for Max to see Jones, but Jones could see him.

His grip tightened on the mallet once more, and his mouth opened to scream, a carnal scream, filled with a mixture of rage and happiness at what was about to happen.

Jones raised the mallet over his head in preparation, and he heard the deadlatch retract from its housing as the knob turned, only to smack back into place.

Jones paused.

The door didn't open.

Had he been seen?

Just then, he heard a siren growing near.

Flashing lights began to filter through the glass panes on the door, followed by the sounds of tires screeching as a police car came to a stop outside of the Henderson household.

FUCK! Jones thought to himself.

Someone must have seen him walk into the house, he thought, cursing the neighbors and wishing violence upon their families.

Jones looked around, searching for a place to hide, getting ready for the police to come barging down the door at any moment to look for him.

He needed to hide.

Jones ran up the stairs as quietly as he could, taking them two at a time.

He made his way into Max's room, then paused at the window. He didn't want to draw attention to himself by moving the curtain, so he tried his best to look through it at the dark shapes in the driveway below.

He heard Max first.

"Can I help you, officer?" Max said.

Jones could see a shape get out of the police car, but he couldn't see who it was exactly. The town was small enough that he could probably identify the officer by name.

"Max Henderson," Chief Frank DeSalvo said. "I have reason to believe that Jones Jepsen is on his way here to kill you."

"What?" Max asked incredulously. "That twerp wouldn't have the balls to kill anyone. What makes you think he's on his way here?"

"Did you have anything to do with what happened to Jones at the graduation ceremony?" the chief asked.

Jones listened closely, trying to hear if Max would admit his guilt.

"Uhh," Max said, sounding a bit flustered. "Nope, wasn't me. I think you've got the wrong guy."

"Right," Frank said, sounding unconvinced. "Well, I believe that Jones is responsible for the deaths of your friends Robby and Carol, among several others. If you had anything to do with him being embarrassed at your graduation, I would assume that you might be next."

"Wait, what the fuck? What do you mean, Carol? Carol is dead?" Max asked.

"I'm sorry to break it to you like this," Frank said.

"I can't believe that. I was just talking to her this morning. A-and you said that he's responsible for killing Robby too?" Max stammered.

"We believe that may be the case," Frank said. "I'm here to keep Jones from killing you as well."

"Ha!" Max exclaimed. "If that little fucker thinks he can take me, then he has another thing coming. If he shows up at my door, I'll be ready for him."

"No," Frank said. "If he shows up here, I will be outside ready to apprehend him. Where are your parents? May I speak with them?"

"They are out of town. I've got the place to myself tonight," Max said.

"Do I have your permission to search the house? I want to secure the premises, to make sure that Jones isn't here," Frank said.

Max hesitated, then let out a deep breath. He waved his hand toward the house.

"Do what you must," he said.

"Fuck!" Jones whispered.

Chapter Thirty-Five

Police Chief Frank DeSalvo opened the door to the Henderson household, stepping into the darkness. He listened for any sound of movement throughout the house, but couldn't hear anything.

He pulled his gun from its holster, pointing it in front of him with one hand as he reached back against the wall. His hand fumbled for a light switch, and he flicked on the lights in the living room. After being in the Burton house, and now this, he realized that he wasn't being paid enough. He felt as though his entire house could fit into the living room of this place, but his job wasn't to judge houses, his job was to catch a murderer.

Frank put his judgment aside and stepped behind the couch, pointing his gun at the space there, and letting out a breath of relief when he found it empty. He wanted to catch Jones as much as the next guy, but he also wasn't too fond of being the only police officer on the scene while a murderer was on the loose.

He knew he should've waited for backup, but he also knew that this was his best chance of catching Jones before he killed another person, and if he didn't catch him soon, the town would have his job.

If anyone were to do this, it had to be him.

He swept the rest of the first floor without any sign of Jones, then stopped at the bottom of the stairs, listening for any signs of movement from the floor above.

Frank took the steps slowly, not wanting to warn Jones that he was coming and give him a chance to prepare. The last thing he needed tonight was to get attacked by a teenage madman.

He made it to the top of the stairs, once more listening for any noise. He opened the door into the master bedroom, leading with his pistol outstretched. He checked under the bed and inside the closet, all of which came up clear.

There was only one room left to check: Max's bedroom.

Frank hesitated outside of the door, much like Jones had done only minutes before, but for different reasons.

Having checked every other room in the house, should Jones be there, this was the only possible room left for him to be in. If anything was going to happen, this was where it would go down.

Frank turned the handle and kicked the door open, staying in the hall in case Jones was to jump out and attack.

Nothing happened.

Frank held the gun with both hands, arms outstretched and stiff in order to keep his aim straight in the event that he fired his gun and it recoiled.

He took a breath, then tread slowly into the room, not bothering to take his eyes off the scene long enough to turn on the light switch.

Frank relied on what little light was coming through the curtains, which was a mix of streetlights and the flashing police lights from his cruiser.

They threw shadows around the area, making it appear like there was someone moving around the room.

Frank tried his best to focus, sweeping the room with his gun. He crouched down and checked under the bed, seeing only a pair of dirty gym socks and a pair of cleats.

That left only the closet.

Frank turned toward it, noting that it was open just a crack.

He pictured Jones inside it, peering out at him, waiting for him to get closer so he could jump out and attack him.

Frank raised the weapon toward the closet.

"Briarwood Police Department! Come out with your hands up!" he shouted.

He waited there motionless, waiting for the door to slowly creak open, revealing the bloodstained figure of Jones Jepsen.

But it never came.

"Briarwood Police Department! Come out with your hands up!" he repeated.

Once again, no response.

He moved forward, inching closer to the door.

His grip tightening on the pistol, he took a deep breath and swung the closet door open.

Just then, a figure leaped out at him, and Frank fired his gun.

Chapter Thirty-Six

F rank yelled, expecting to be battered to pieces by Jones. But the attack never came.

Frank had fallen to the ground, and someone had fallen on top of him.

Or so he thought.

He got to his feet, uninjured, and ran over to the light switch.

What he saw almost made him laugh at himself.

What he had thought was a person in the closet had just been Max's football uniform. His helmet had been stacked on his shoulder pads and it had given off the impression that it was a person. Max had shoved his closet so full of stuff that it wouldn't close, hence why it was cracked open. When Frank had opened the door, everything had come tumbling out at him.

Frank looked down at the Briarwood High football uniform, which now had a bullet hole through it.

The department would likely garnish his paycheck to pay for that one, he thought to himself.

Jones wasn't here.

Frank walked over to the window, looking down at his cruiser on the street.

He didn't see Jones from his point of view, which was a good sign.

Frank turned around and walked out of the room.

What he didn't know was that Jones had opened the window in Max's bedroom and climbed out onto the porch roof. He was currently straddled against the wall beside the window, waiting for his moment.

Jones could hear Max on the porch underneath him, crying over Carol.

Max sniffled, before jumping when the front door opened behind him.

It was only Frank.

"Can I go inside now?" Max asked.

"Fine," Frank said, holstering his weapon. "But be vigilant. My cruiser will be parked just outside. If you hear or see anything, you just let me know, and I will come inside."

"Right," Max said. He opened the door and walked inside, not even bothering to say goodbye to Frank.

Max locked the front door, pausing a moment as he did so.

He still couldn't believe that Carol was dead, and who knew that Jones would have the balls to do such a thing?

Frank turned away from the door and walked back to his cruiser. Once he reached his vehicle, he placed his hand on the handle, but stopped there. He turned back to look at the window where Max's bedroom was, but there was no one there.

Max dropped his keys on the table and then looked around the house. Nothing was out of place, but something just didn't feel right to him. He knew that the officer had just searched his home and didn't find anything, but it still didn't fix the queasiness in his stomach.

Max walked up to his room and was surprised to find his football equipment scattered all over the place.

He bent over, picking up his equipment and cursing the officer for treating his room like a pigsty and not bothering to clean up his mess.

Max brought his stuff over to the closet to put it away, and when he opened the door, his blood ran cold.

There stood Jones Jepsen, a wicked smile plastered across his face as he looked at the expression of horror on Max's own. His face was covered in specks of blood left over from Carol, and the mallet he held in his hands was dripping with the stuff.

Max stepped backward, and Jones stepped over some equipment in the closet to get to him.

Jones wasn't in any rush. He knew the police officer was looking for him outside and wouldn't expect him to be in the house that he had just checked over. Besides, Jones had been dreaming about this night for years.

"You!" Max said.

"Me," Jones said, baring his teeth in a smile.

Suddenly, something happened that Jones wasn't expecting.

Max rushed toward him.

Jones tried to raise the mallet over his head to swing, but he didn't have the time to.

Max tackled Jones to the ground, and his mallet went clambering away on the carpeted floor.

Max now had a smile of his own, as he stood up, planting his foot down on Jones's chest, pinning him to the floor.

Was Max going to go to the police? Turn in the guy who had killed Carol and Robby?

Jones was furious at what Max had done for him, and he desperately wanted to end the boy's life, but deep down there was still a part of him that held fear for his bully.

And rightfully so.

While Jones was pinned down, Max slapped on his helmet and shoulder pads as if he was getting ready for a game.

"So you've decided that you wanted to kill me and my friends,"

Max said. He tightened the straps on his helmet. "Alright. I'd like to see you try."

Then he did something very unexpected. He stepped off of Jones's chest, allowing him the chance to get up.

Jones got to his feet, feeling naked without his mallet by his side.

Max then stepped in between Jones and the mallet, and he took the stance of a linebacker getting ready for the snap. He shoved his mouthguard between his teeth, then bared them at Jones, his expression taking on a look of glee that made Jones wonder which of them was supposed to be the crazy one.

Jones lurched toward the mallet, and a second later he was lying flat on his back, the wind knocked out of him as Max tackled him to the floor.

"AGAIN!" Max screamed through his mouthguard, just inches from Jones's face.

Max got back to his feet like nothing happened, taking up his stance once again in the center of the room.

Jones hesitantly got to his feet, clutching his stomach.

He had come here to kill Max, and instead, he was involved in some sick game of cat and mouse with the boy, which would ultimately lead to one of their deaths.

"Come at me, boy!" Max yelled, bending over and pawing at the ground with one of his feet.

Jones stared at Max, who was practically growling through his mouthguard at this point. He just knew that the boy had to be on something, there was no way that anyone could have this amount of energy naturally.

Jones matched Max's stance, thinking that he had seen it in enough football games that it must give the player some kind of tactical advantage.

He leaped forward once again, and once more, Max had him splayed out on the ground in seconds, crying out in pain as his muscles reacted like he had been hit by a truck.

"WOOH!" Max yelled. "That one was for Robby! AGAIN!"

Max was effectively using Jones as a tackling dummy.

Jones was getting really tired of this game. The more they played it, the more he hated this guy, and he made a note in his mind to inflict as much physical pain on Max as possible while the boy was still alive.

Jones lined up in front of Max once again, this time thinking back to the one football game he had watched while he was in school. He was there to pick up his girlfriend, who was cheerleading at the time, and he had stayed long enough to watch a few plays. He hadn't understood them at the time, but right about now, he felt the need to implement some of the things he had seen the players do.

Jones bent down, keeping his toes planted on the carpet, and letting just the fingertips of one hand touch the floor. He kept his other hand elevated behind him like a sprinter getting ready to launch.

At this angle, Jones could see his mallet on the floor behind Max. He made a mental note of its location, then planned a strategy to get to it.

Max was raring to go, his body shaking with the excitement of this game to the death. He was a good football player, and he was waiting for his opponent to make the first move.

This time, Jones was ready for him.

He swung his arm forward as he pushed off the ground with his toes, launching himself forward.

Max did the same from where he stood, putting his hands forward to grab Jones in the chest and shove him back.

However, this time Jones wasn't going to fall for that.

Jones moved to his right, sending Max in that direction, and at the last moment, Jones shifted all of his weight to his left and moved in the opposite direction.

Max hadn't expected this type of move from someone as unathletic as Jones, and he ended up falling forward, crashing onto the carpet with his face.

Jones used this time wisely, diving forward and picking up his mallet.

Jones got to his feet, feeling empowered once more as he spun the mallet in his hands.

He paused as Max stood up, turning around and seeing Jones waiting for him with a mallet. But Jones didn't strike, instead, he gestured toward Max to stand up and get into his position.

Max harumphed at the idea, as if Jones thought that he could take him. Max got back into his stance, angrier now that he had been bested by the boy whom he had been picking on for years.

This time Max was on offense.

He ran at Jones with everything he had, but Jones was getting rather good at swinging a mallet.

Jones ran forward, meeting Max in the middle of the room, swinging his mallet from below. The end of it swung up and connected with Max's pads where his ribs would have been. The force of the shock sent Max on his ass, clutching the area where he had been hit.

Jones looked down on him with a smile, and as Max met his gaze, there was a look in his eye that acknowledged that the tables had turned.

Max was now the underdog in this fight.

And he needed to run.

Chapter Thirty-Seven

Jones watched as Max's eyes darted to the door and back to Jones. He knew that Max was going to run. He would let him. Jones couldn't be more interested in playing cat and mouse with his bully. He thought back to all the times that Max and his friends had chased him through the halls of their high school. All the times that Jones had begged people for help, students, teachers, and none of them did a thing. No one would stop the boys from doing whatever they wanted to Jones, and now there was nothing stopping him from doing the same to Max.

Jones stepped closer to Max, looking down on the boy with a wicked grin.

"Run."

Max didn't have to be told twice.

He raced to his feet as fast as he could, which was a problem as he didn't recognize how hurt he truly was.

Max immediately collapsed, clutching his ribs which he now realized were broken. This was going to be more difficult than he thought.

Max turned to see Jones strolling slowly toward him, mallet

leaning on his shoulder like a baseball player walking to home plate. He knew he needed to move quickly or something terrible would be done to him.

It's what he would do if he were in Jones's shoes.

Max got on all fours, not bothering to waste time standing up. He still felt pain in his ribs, but it was less painful after distributing some of his weight to his knees.

He zombie crawled toward the stairs, not checking to see what Jones was doing behind him.

Max stopped once he reached the top of the landing, looking down at the daunting drop beneath him.

He was thankful that he had taken the time to put on his helmet and pads, and he knew what he had to do.

Max slid his body forward, over the top of the first step.

Gravity did its part, and before he knew it, he was sliding face-first down the stairs, his helmet taking the brunt of the damage as it hit every step on the way down.

Just before he got to the bottom, he hit one of the stairs differently than he should have, and his body flipped over several times, slamming his back into the wall at the bottom landing with a loud thud.

Max was slumped against the wall, trying to catch his breath, when he noticed movement out of the corner of his eye.

He looked up and saw Jones smirking at the top of the stairs.

Jones paused to admire the sorry state that his next victim was in, then he started to slowly descend the stairs, one step at a time. He didn't want to end Max's suffering immediately, rather, he wanted to relish in the boy's fear and know that his death came slowly.

Max could feel his heart beating faster than it had during any football game.

He began to crawl away from the stairwell as fast as he could, making his way toward the window.

Max could hear the sound of Jones's boots coming slowly down the steps.

Clomp. Clomp. Clomp.

Max was almost to the window, every movement sending a wave of nauseating pain through his body. He looked back, not seeing Jones behind him.

He shuffled the last few feet to the window, working through the pain to lift himself up to the sill.

Max almost passed out from the effort, but in the end, he was rewarded with the sight of Frank's police car sitting outside.

He banged on the window, trying to get the man's attention, but no matter how much he tried, the door never opened.

Max was starting to give up when he saw Jones's reflection in the window.

He spun around to see the kid he once bullied towering over him.

"Crying for help, are we? How does it feel knowing that nobody is coming to help you no matter how much you scream?" Jones asked, reveling in the moment.

Jones swung his mallet low and from the side, like a golfer driving a ball across the fairway. He drove the mallet into the side of Max's kneecap, shattering it and causing the bone to splinter.

Max screamed in pain, instinctively grabbing his knee, which only made him cry out even more.

But Jones didn't want to finish him off there. The last thing he needed was for someone to see them from the road and try to play hero.

Jones grabbed Max by the foot, making sure to grab the one from the damaged leg. From there he twisted and pulled, yanking Max away from the window and dragging him into the kitchen.

Max pawed at the ground, trying to get a handful of something to stop himself from being pulled, but he only managed to rip up parts of the carpet as they moved.

Finally, Jones pulled Max's body to the kitchen, making the boy sit up with his back against one of the cabinets.

"Please don't hurt me, I'll do anything you want!" Max begged.

Jones looked at Max and sneered, he was so pitiful when he begged.

Jones went back to what he was doing, looking through the kitchen drawers for things that he could use to torture Max. He tore out drawer after drawer, sending them to the floor if they didn't have what he wanted, covering the floor in spices and oven mitts.

"Ah, here we go," Jones said. He had opened a drawer that contained the silverware.

Jones pulled out a handful, containing a mixture of forks, spoons, and butter knives.

He held them up in front of his eyes, inspecting them.

"These will do nicely," Jones said. "But which one should I use first? Hmm." He pointed to each of the implements in his hand. "Eenie, meenie, miny, mo. This one!"

Jones pulled a butter knife out from the collection, then grabbed one of Max's hands and held it against the cabinet.

"What are you doing? What are you going to do with tha..." Max's statement was cut short as Jones shoved the butter knife through the palm of Max's hand, lodging it into the cabinet door behind it.

Max screamed in pain, staring at the blood running down his injured hand. He would never be able to play football again, Max thought.

While Max was distracted with his hand, Jones grabbed the other one and quickly shoved another knife into the other hand, likewise pinning it to the cabinet on the other side of the boy.

Max screamed once more, and he spit at Jones as tears ran down his face.

Between the blood and the tears, and the veins seemingly about to pop in Max's face, he looked like Jesus Christ on the cross getting an exorcism, Jones thought.

He liked the idea of that, but he wasn't done with him yet.

"Fuck you, you fucking..." Max's curses came to a halt as Jones grabbed the tip of his tongue and shoved the tines of a fork through it as far as it could go.

Blood began to pour from Max's mouth, and he tried to scream, but screaming only caused his tongue muscles to move, which put him in even more pain. The fork sticking out of it made it so he couldn't pull his tongue back into his mouth, so he was forced to keep his tongue sticking out like an eight-year-old kid. He was in so much pain already, and he couldn't imagine what Jones had in store for him next.

He couldn't help but wonder where the fuck the cop was that was supposed to be looking out for Jones. Did he not see them through the window? Could he not hear his screams?

He stared up at Jones with hate in his eyes, wishing nothing but death upon his torturer.

Jones smiled back at Max, and that's when held up the spoon.

Max didn't know what he meant to do with that, but then it hit him, and his eyes went wide with fear.

"Good boy. Just like that," Jones said.

Max's body thrashed this way and that, but his knee was busted and his hands were pinned to the cabinets, and there was nothing he could do as Jones stuck the edge of the spoon under his eyelid, and scooped it out.

At that point, Max couldn't take the pain anymore, and he passed out.

Jones took the eye over to the fridge and placed it inside the egg carton for his family to find later. Then he turned back to Max.

He slapped the boy's face repeatedly until he woke up. His head swirled around, realizing that this wasn't a dream. His one good eye looked up at Jones and he screamed one last time.

"NUHHH!" Max screamed through the fork in his tongue.

Then Jones brought the end of the mallet upon his helmet, leaving an indent that caved in the boy's skull.

Jones watched as the blood began to pour out of the helmet where Max's brain had been squished. In doing so, he had failed to see the men coming toward the front door. They could see him, but he hadn't seen them.

Suddenly, the front door flew open, crashing into the drywall behind it.

"Briarwood Police Department!"

Jones looked up, and his eyes met with those of Chief Frank DeSalvo.

Then he made a break for it.

"Stop! Put your hands up!" Frank said as Jones got closer to the back door. "I'm warning you! I will shoot!"

Jones remembered feeling like someone had stuck a hot poker through his chest. He felt the shot before he heard it. Then his body fell through the sliding glass door.

Frank ran over to the kitchen, where he found Max nailed to the cabinet like the body of Christ. He knew it was futile, but he still bent down and felt for a pulse.

There was none.

"Can I get some officers to the Henderson house? I have shots fired. I repeat, shots fired. One victim so far, and I have Jones Jepsen," Frank said.

He could hear a cheer going up in the background as someone radioed that they were on their way.

It was hard for him to look away from Max's body, and he couldn't imagine having to break the news of his death to his parents, especially since he was supposed to be guarding the house. He had no explanation other than the fact that he was watching the front of the house and expecting Jones to come from the outside rather than the inside. He had messed up royally, and he was hoping that with the capture of Jones Jepsen, he would be lucky if he could get away with keeping his job.

Jones Jepsen.

He had almost forgotten about him.

Frank stood up and strolled to the back door, which now lay in pieces all over the ground.

He could see blood from Jones's bullet wound, indicating that he had landed the shot.

But Jones was nowhere to be seen.

Chapter Thirty-Eight

Jones lumbered through the woods behind Max's house. At one point he turned and saw the distinct outline of Chief Frank DeSalvo standing in the light of the sliding glass doorway. He was too far away to make out specific features of the man. Either that or he had already lost so much blood that his vision was beginning to get blurry.

The pain in his chest was searing, and every time his arms swayed it sent a volley of pain signals to his brain.

The bullet from Frank's gun had missed his heart by inches, but Jones could feel the blood coursing down his shirt. At this rate, he wasn't going to make it to his next destination.

Jones had unfinished business. He felt like his time on this earth was coming to an end, but before it did, he wanted to take out all the people who had caused him harm over the years.

The only one left was Kyle.

Jones took another step, and he felt his leg wobble beneath him.

He collapsed to his knees, staring up at the stars peeking through the treetops. His vision was getting worse, and the real stars were soon replaced with fake ones as he began to lose blood at a rapid rate.

Jones ripped off a chunk of his jacket and used it to staunch the bleeding, hoping his blood would clot. He pressed it against the hole in his chest, and the responding pain made him scream in agony.

"Just. One. More," Jones said through clenched teeth. He took one step up and collapsed again.

Jones pressed his forehead to the ground and screamed into the earth. He lay there, panting, wanting nothing more than to finish his conquest.

He didn't know what else to do. After all of the crimes he had committed, there sure wasn't a place for him in heaven. Praying to god wouldn't help him now.

If he couldn't get into heaven, maybe there was a place for him in hell.

Jones grabbed his chest with his hand, covering it in fresh blood. With an angry war cry, he shoved his bloody hand into the dirt.

"Just let me get one more. Just one more! I am willing to pledge my eternal soul to Satan, if you let me get just one more. I need to end his life, and then you can have mine."

Jones's vision drifted slowly into darkness as he lost consciousness, but just before he did so, he swore he saw something crawl out of the ground and grab his bloody hand.

Then everything went black.

Chapter Thirty-Nine

"Is Kyle there?" a gravelly voice said on the phone. "Yes he is, may I ask who is calling?" Kyle's mother asked.

"It's Chief Frank DeSalvo. I really need to speak with Kyle," Frank said.

"What did he do?" Kyle's mother asked.

"Nothing ma'am. Well...nothing to be concerned about right now. I just need to talk to him, and then I'll let him fill you in on the details later. I don't have enough time right now to repeat myself," Frank said.

"I'll get him," she said. "Kyle! There's someone on the phone who wants to speak with you!"

"Tell them to leave a message, my program is on!" Kyle shouted from the other room.

"Kyle Matthew! You get in this room this very instant!" his mother shouted.

She could hear him sighing dramatically from the living room as if it was such a burden on his life to answer the phone when somebody called for him.

Kyle entered the kitchen, rolling his eyes at his mother, who handed him the phone and then folded her arms.

"Well? Aren't you going to give me some privacy?" Kyle asked.

"Not for this call I'm not," she said.

A confused look crossed Kyle's face. This was a pretty unusual way for his mother to act. Normally, when he got a phone call it would be from one of the guys or from Carol, and his mother would go into another room to give him some space.

Kyle brought the phone slowly up to his ear.

"Hello?" he said.

"Kyle? This is Chief Frank DeSalvo. I'm calling you from Max's house tonight. I've got some bad news to give you, and you're going to want to be sitting down for this. Are you sitting down?"

Kyle moved one of the dining room chairs back and forth, to make it sound like he was taking a seat, however, he remained standing, his mother watching him like a hawk.

"Yeah, I'm sitting down," Kyle said, rolling his eyes.

"I don't know how to break this to you kid, but I've been getting quite a lot of practice recently. All of your friends are dead," Frank said.

"Is this some kind of a sick joke?" Kyle said. "Did Max put you up to this?" Kyle smirked at the idea of Max doing something like this, and in his head, he was plotting ways to get his friend back for this.

"I'm afraid it's no joke. It appears that Jones Jepsen is responsible for the death of your friend Robby, and earlier today he claimed the lives of your friends Carol and Max. It is my belief that he is carrying out these murders in response to a prank that your friend group pulled on him during your graduation ceremony. Now, I wasn't against pulling the occasional prank when I was in high school, but this has gotten way out of hand. Jones has gotten away once again, and I believe that he is en route to your residence as we speak. All of my officers are busy collecting evidence at all of the crime scenes left behind by Jones tonight. I will be on my way to you as soon as I can, but in the meantime, I would advise that you lock all of your doors and windows. Jones is to be considered armed and highly dangerous," Frank said.

"Wait. You're serious about all this?" Kyle asked.

"Deathly."

Kyle turned away from his mother.

"All of my friends are dead?"

"Yes."

Kyle hung the phone back on the wall. The sound of it echoed around the silent room as his mother waited for him to fill her in on what the call was about.

The realization of what the chief had said hit him then.

Jones was on his way there to kill him.

Kyle ran out of the kitchen, locking every window that he passed, and drawing the curtains closed so nobody could see what was happening on the inside. If Jones were to show up, Kyle wanted him to think that nobody was home.

"What on earth are you doing?" his mother asked.

"I've got no time to explain!" Kyle said, bolting the door shut.

"Well somebody ought to start doing some explaining around here. Stop!" his mother shouted, grabbing him by the shoulders. "What's going on?"

Kyle couldn't meet her gaze. He felt that the moment he did so, he would start crying, and he didn't want to seem like a wimp right now. His eyes kept darting to the windows as if waiting for Jones's face to pop up behind them.

"I, I sort of pulled a prank on a kid from school. He didn't take it well, and he, well, he killed my friends and he's coming here next," Max said.

His mother pulled him in for a hug, and he couldn't help but cry like a baby into his mother's shoulder for a few seconds.

"Barricade the door."

Kyle's father was working on the back door, so he enlisted his little brother Brian to help him with the front. Together they were able to move the heavy, solid wood coffee table in front of the door.

The family waited in silence for what felt like hours but probably wasn't that long. They had turned the TV off, along with all of the lights in the house. If they wanted Jones to believe that nobody was home, they would have to sell it.

Kyle knew that Chief DeSalvo was doing the best he could, heading a search party through the woods behind Max's house to find Jones, and he hoped they found him quickly.

It took all he could not to pick up the phone and make a call to the police station every thirty seconds to see if they caught him.

The family was huddled together in the living room, with Brian and his mother sitting on the couch. Kyle and his father paced the room, as quietly as they could, alert for any sound they heard.

Several times they jumped as the branches from the apple tree in the front yard scraped along the windows of the house. Kyle told himself that if they ever got out of this predicament, he was going to chop that thing down.

It was pitch black inside, with the only light coming from the moonlight shining through the window curtains.

It was so quiet that Kyle could hear the differences in breathing between his family members.

Suddenly, a loud, maniacal cackle erupted from outside.

Kyle's blood froze in his veins as he realized that Jones was outside.

He didn't need a light to see that his family's eyes were wide open, staring in fear at the doors and windows around them, wondering where Jones would make his move.

They saw the outline of Jones through the window curtains as he walked around the house. There was a loud scratching noise, like nails on a chalkboard, as Jones dragged his fingernails along the glass as he walked.

There were bouts of silence, followed by the sound of furious knocking, as Jones tested the windows around the house, rocking the frames back and forth to try to knock them off their tracks.

"I'm coming for you, Kyle!" Jones screamed from the side of the home.

The family turned to face that side of the house, when suddenly they heard footsteps on the front porch.

Thud. Thud. Thud. Thud.

The sound stopped at the front door, and the family turned toward it, holding their breath in fear of being heard by this deranged serial killer.

The door handle shook as he tested it. Furious that he couldn't get it open, Jones shoved the handle back and forth, rocking the door on its hinges as he tried to break it off.

The shaking suddenly stopped, and for a moment, the family thought that Jones had left.

That's when the knocking started.

Knock. Knock. Knock.

The family didn't move.

"Aren't you going to let me in? It's pretty rude to leave a guest standing outside on the porch," Jones said, his voice calm, as if he hadn't just tried to break in.

Once again, the family didn't move.

Kyle found himself praying that Chief DeSalvo would walk up behind Jones and shoot him.

Knock. Knock. Knock.

"I'm still out here," Jones said. "Why won't you let me in? Then we could talk like civilized beings and discuss the sins you have wrought against me."

Nobody budged.

KNOCK. KNOCK. KNOCK.

"If you don't let me in, then not only am I going to kill you, but I will also kill your whole family. How does that sound?"

Kyle made a move toward the door, but his father stopped him in his tracks, forcing him to stand his ground.

A few moments went by before Jones spoke again.

"No? So be it. Just like your friends, your family's deaths will be on your conscience, and I will make sure that you hear their screams as they lay dying just before I kill you."

Brian began to cry out of fear, and his mother quickly shoved her hand over his mouth.

"I heard that," Jones said. He leaned against the door and tapped on it with one finger like a school girl on the phone with her crush. "I know you're in there. Just let me in. Let me in, and this will all be over very soon, with minimal casualties."

Once again, nobody moved, and Jones's patience seemed to be put past the edge.

It was as if a switch had been flipped, and a totally different Jones appeared, one that Kyle had never dealt with, otherwise, he would have never bullied the kid.

Just then, the door rocked on its hinges as if it were hit by a wrecking ball. Jones had hit it with his mallet, putting all of his weight behind it to try to break down the door.

"LET!" BANG. "ME!" BANG. "IN!" BANG.

The door was beginning to shift with every blow it received.

As they watched, the nails holding the hinges to the door frame slowly began to inch their way out, clattering to the floor one by one.

Suddenly the top half of the door snapped, folding inward in a splintery mess as it fell upon the coffee table below. Jones shoved his head in through the hole, turning to see the family huddled in the living room.

"Boo."

Kyle, Brian, and their mother ran in fear, each of them scattering to someplace in the house where they felt safest. There was no sense of preservation of family, it was every man for themselves.

Their father was the only person who stood his ground, moving closer to the door to confront Jones head-on, to try to protect his family one last time.

"You are not welcome here," Kyle's father said. "I suggest that you leave at once, before I-"

Those were the last words Kyle's father ever uttered.

Before he could react, Jones swung his mallet through the opening in the door and caved in the man's skull.

He seemed to fall in slow motion, collapsing to his knees before toppling over onto the floor.

Kyle choked down a scream as he heard his father's last words. He had run upstairs and hid inside the hallway closet. He wished that he had paid attention to where the rest of his family had gone, but it was too late for that now. If he were to move and try to find one of them now, he would definitely alert Jones to his location, and it would result in his immediate demise.

Jones stepped through what was left of the door, moving his head from side to side, releasing a satisfying cracking sound as he did so.

After he finished stretching, he bent down and removed the end of his mallet from the skull of Kyle's father.

Jones shook some of the blood off, then got to work, making his way through the bottom floor of the house.

His search of the kitchen and the living room yielded no results, but as he walked closer to the door to the laundry room, he could hear the whimpers of somebody inside.

Jones bowed his head, then shook it as disappointment overtook him. He was unsatisfied with how easy they were making this for him.

Using one finger, he pushed open the laundry room door, at which point the whimpers turned into sobs.

The laundry room was simple, with one side containing a window facing the backyard, and the other side having a washing machine and dryer, with a shelf overhead to hold detergent.

Jones walked to the other end of the room, where he found Kyle's mother crouched behind the dryer.

He shook his head once more, then grabbed her by the hair and dragged her out of the room. She kicked and screamed the whole way, finally giving him some fight, but it wasn't enough to overpower him.

For some reason tonight he felt like he was filled with a sense of energy he never had before. After he had passed out, his body had recovered slightly from the bullet wound. It had clotted up finally, and when he awoke he found that he was able to stand without falling down, and his vision had returned to normal. However, he felt a surge of energy like never before, like he was an old man filled with the blood of a teenager, able to do things he had never thought of. He felt like he could walk through walls and lift vehicles. He would love to test out that theory, but for now, he had business to take care of.

Jones dragged Kyle's mother into the living room, and she broke down in tears after seeing her husband's lifeless body on the floor.

He held her there, forcing her head straight so she couldn't look anywhere else but at her dead husband.

"You see that?" Jones said, shoving her face a little closer. "That is the result of your bad parenting. That is what happens when you raise an asshole like Kyle. Shit like this happens."

Jones turned to face the stairs.

"I have your mother down here Kyle. Your father, well, let's just say he couldn't make it tonight. But your mother is down here and she really wants you to come downstairs. If you don't come downstairs in the next thirty seconds, I will kill your mother. The clock starts now."

Kyle's mother screamed, begging for her life.

"Oh no, no, no. Please don't kill me. I'll do anything. Just don't kill me," she pleaded.

Jones looked down at her with disgust. Right now she was a pawn in his little game, but he couldn't wait until he could shut her the hell up.

He waited impatiently, but nothing happened.

"You hear that?" Jones said, giving Kyle's mother's hair a tug.

She stopped her whimpering for a moment, and they both listened intently.

There was nothing.

No sounds of police coming, and no sounds of footsteps from upstairs.

Her children weren't coming to her rescue.

They were too afraid of Jones to risk their lives, even if it meant saving their mother's.

Jones frowned at the stairwell.

"It's a pity," Jones said. "I really hoped that would work. However, the show must go on, and you've been cut."

Kyle's mother screamed one last time, then surprisingly, Jones let her go.

She immediately began to crawl away, passing through the puddle of blood made by her husband.

Jones even let her go a few feet, allowing her some hope that he would let her survive.

Then he brought the mallet down on the back of her head, sending her face into the ground so hard that the front of it caved in, making the rest of her skull flush against the floor.

"I'm sorry to tell you this boys, but your mother is no longer with us. Player two has been knocked out of the game, and now it's your turn to play."

Kyle was doing his best to hold back his tears from inside the hallway closet. He had pulled a prank on Jones, and because of his actions, now both of his parents were dead. He still hadn't seen his little brother, but he hoped that he would be okay. Kyle was still too afraid to move from where he was.

The hallway closet had slatted doors, similar to the one that Jones had hidden in while at Robby's house.

Through the slats, Kyle could make out the doors to each of the bedrooms, and at the end of the hall, he could see the top of the stairs.

Suddenly, a light turned on downstairs, illuminating the stairwell.

Thud. Thud. Thud.

Kyle held his breath as he heard Jones making his way slowly up the stairs.

It was like he was moving slowly deliberately, as if he wanted to build suspense, to send their hearts racing before he got to them. It truly was a game to him, and he was having fun.

Thud. Thud. Thud.

Kyle could see Jones's shadow on the wall opposing the stairs.

It was getting smaller as Jones moved farther away from the light. It grew more detailed, and Kyle could make out the shape of a mallet in his hands.

Then suddenly, Jones arrived at the top of the stairs.

He stopped to take in a deep whiff of the air, as if he could smell the boys.

Then he looked directly at the hallway closet, as if he knew exactly where Kyle was.

Kyle felt like Jones was staring at him directly in the eyes.

They stood like that for a moment, none of them willing to blink.

Then Jones began to walk slowly down the hall toward him.

He started to whistle a tune as he went, slinging his mallet over his shoulder.

"Oh where, oh where, could the little boy be," Jones sang out, then he made a left turn, skipping Kyle altogether and walking directly into Brian's room.

Brian was hiding under the bed, which was a first for him at night. He had always been afraid of monsters under his bed, but for once, he was pretty sure the monsters were outside the bed. At this moment in particular, the monster was roaming the house.

He heard the screams of his parents, and he was too afraid to come out when Jones asked them to. What was he supposed to do? He was only eleven, he couldn't take on a serial killer on a rampage with a weapon.

Instead, he huddled under the bed and held his hands to his ears, blocking out the sound, which is why he was so surprised when he removed them and he heard whistling outside of his bedroom.

Suddenly, footsteps raced into his room, and as he watched, muddy boots stomped closer and closer to the bed where he hid, leaving bloody footprints in their wake.

Stomp. Stomp. STOMP.

The boots came to a stop in front of Brian's bed.

He held his hand in front of his mouth, trying to prevent himself from being heard, otherwise he was pretty sure he would be screaming at the top of his lungs.

Just then, the boots disappeared one by one, and Brian felt the bed springs above his head compress as Jones climbed on top of it.

Jones began to jump on the bed, getting higher and higher, and the more weight he put on the bed, the closer it came to crushing Brian below.

"Oh where, oh where, could the little boy be, OH WHERE, OH WHERE COULD HE BE?" Jones sang, screaming out the lyrics at the end.

Finally, Brian couldn't take it anymore, and he scrambled out from under the bed, making a break for the door.

Then he felt a hand on the back of his shirt.

"Gotcha," Jones said with a smile.

Kyle's ears rang as his little brother's scream pierced his eardrums.

Then almost as quickly as it began, the scream cut off sickeningly.

Kyle placed his hands over his mouth to stifle his cries.

He could still hear the echo of his little brother's scream as it made its final pass through the house.

His little brother was dead because of him.

His whole family was dead because of him.

Kyle heard a smack as his little brother's body hit the floor.

It took everything he had in him not to break down crying, giving away his position.

Then something happened that distracted him from thoughts of his brother.

Jones appeared in the doorway of his little brother's room, wiping a sheet of blood from the end of his mallet.

Kyle peered through the slats of the door, watching as Jones moved into his parent's room. He heard Jones tossing things around, throwing furniture in his quest to find him. He watched as Jones walked passed his hiding spot to get to his room.

His room was on the same wall as the closet doors, so he wasn't able to see him go in from his angle.

Kyle pressed his face against the slats, trying to see as much as possible.

Suddenly, Jones's face appeared in the slats, his eyes meeting Kyle's.

"Boo," he said, opening the door.

Chapter Forty

Chief Frank DeSalvo showed up at Kyle's house later that night. He was exhausted, having just combed through the woods between Max and Kyle's house and found nothing but blood stains in the trees.

Jones was nowhere to be found.

Kyle's house was the next place on his list. He had to make sure that the family was safe. It was the last thing he had to do that night, and then he would go home and crawl into bed.

His plan was to knock on the door, make sure the family was still alright, and then post an officer at the front door, similar to what he had done at Max's house. It was standard protocol in this situation, though usually, the officer stationed outside would be able to subdue the suspect before they got inside. He had to admit, he had messed up on that one, and he expected to hear about it from his superiors in the morning.

He would have to answer to the town, and the mayor would have his ass once he found out that Frank was so close to Jones and still let one of Robby's friends get murdered under his nose.

Frank had brought another squad car behind him, just in case he needed backup. He also brought them along in case he needed to leave a car here to protect the family.

He pulled up in front of Kyle's house and immediately knew that something was wrong.

The front door was not only smashed in, it was folded in half, with the top part of it missing, leaving a gaping black hole where it should have been.

Frank got out of his squad car, taking his gun from its sheath. He hunched over, gun stretched out in front of him as he made his way around his car.

He motioned for the other officers to get out of their car and check out the perimeter of the house.

"Do me a favor, look through the windows, and tell me if you see anything," Frank whispered to one of his officers.

Frank stood at the bottom of the porch, waiting for his deputy to get back to him.

The officer moved to each of the windows, trying to peer through, but he was unsuccessful. The house was too dark to see inside.

Frank made his way slowly up the stairs. He approached the doorway with caution, gun first. He pointed it through the gap where the top of the door should have been, motioning it left and right as he looked in.

The house was pitch black, and a quick test of a light switch inside the doorway let him know that power to the house had been cut.

Chief Frank DeSalvo motioned for one of the other officers to go first, then he would cover his rear.

The other officer pulled out his flashlight and led the way inside. His arms were crossed at the wrist, one hand holding his flashlight, the other holding his standard-issue pistol.

As he entered the dwelling, his nose detected a familiar smell. The air was filled with a coppery musk.

He got two steps into the house, and his light caught something on the floor. Pointing it at the ground, he saw a trail of blood etched into the carpet. It appeared as if a struggle had happened in this spot, and then a body had been dragged away, down the hall and around the corner.

The officer nodded back to Frank, pointing out his findings. Frank whispered quietly into his radio, calling for backup. Then he joined the officer inside.

Together, the men followed the trail of blood, careful not to step in any in an effort not to contaminate the crime scene.

As they continued, the scene only worsened.

Blood was splattered on the walls in a pattern that was consistent with a swinging motion. They walked into another room and were met with the beginnings of yet another trail of blood, this one going in the same direction as the previous one. They could now see handprints on the wall where a second victim had tried to prevent themselves from being dragged away. They could also tell from the handprints where the victim had stopped resisting, potentially after receiving another blow from the intruder.

The younger officer had to pull his handkerchief out of his pocket and bring it to his face. The smell of blood had grown even stronger as they moved closer to the center of the house. Between that and the bloody scene in front of him, it was all he could do not to vomit all over the carpet. He had been an officer for a few years and had thought that he had seen some bad stuff, but nothing had compared to what he was seeing now. Briarwood was a peaceful town, where nothing bad ever seemed to happen. The worst that he had seen was the aftermath of a car accident that had left a local boy dead from blunt-force trauma to the head.

This was worse.

Much worse.

Taking a deep breath to steady himself, he knew he must go on. He pocketed the handkerchief and raised his flashlight once more in front of him.

They walked passed the stairwell, where another trail of blood could be seen coming down the stairs. It pooled on several steps and dripped onto the stairs below it.

Instead of checking out the upstairs, they decided to follow where the new blood trail converged into the ones they were already following.

That's when they heard the singing.

"Ring around the Rosie," a voice rang out from the other room.

They stepped around a corner into the living room, where they were met with a ghastly sight.

Jones had dragged the chairs from the dining room into the living room. He had arranged them into a circle, with each chair facing each other.

The trails of blood belonged to each of the house's residents, whose bodies were splayed out in the chairs.

The young officer had to run out of the house to vomit. There was no getting over what he was seeing here.

This wasn't a normal murder. Heck, this wasn't a normal serial killing.

"Pockets full of posies," the voice sang out.

Jones had had his fun with each of the bodies, taking swings to each of their body parts with his mallet. The human body contained 206 bones, and he strived to break every one of them.

The family's bodies were beaten up and bruised, swollen in every place imaginable. In some places, the bones had been splintered to the point where fragments of them stuck through the skin.

Their limbs were bent at unnatural angles and a young boy's arm had been broken to the point where it curved in a spiral.

The faces of all the victims were rendered unrecognizable, having been bashed in with a mallet to the point where the viewer could observe the contents of their skulls.

The bodies were as white as bone, and their blood poured from countless wounds onto the floor.

This was where the police found Jones Jepsen.

"Ashes, ashes," Jones sang, his head raised to the ceiling.

Jones 1963

Jones was sitting on the floor in the middle of the family.

There he was completely covered in his victim's blood. He wore a wicked grin on his face that stretched from ear to ear. He didn't even seem to notice when the police came in, he was too busy playing in his victim's blood.

As Frank watched in horror, Jones placed his finger in the puddle of blood, then placed his other hand on a bare stretch of carpet. Jones then used his blood-covered finger to trace an outline of his hand into the carpet, like he was making a drawing of a turkey on Thanksgiving.

Jones then raised his hands to the moonlight pouring in from a nearby window. He smiled as he examined the strands of blood that strung between his fingers as he outstretched them.

"We all fall down," Jones said, his eyes meeting with Frank's.

Frank stood there in shock, mouth hanging wide open as his brain tried to process what he was seeing. He didn't even move as the backup he had ordered earlier arrived and took Jones into custody.

As Jones was escorted into the back of a police car, frightened neighbors watched the scene unfold through their curtained windows.

The next day the newspaper was plastered with the headline "Serial killer caught!" and featured a picture of Jones Jepsen on the front page. He was sitting in the back of a police cruiser, his hand-cuffed wrists held up in front of his face. His hands were covered in blood, and he seemed not to notice the commotion going on around him. Instead, his eyes were wide, focused only on the blood smeared between his fingers. A smile graced his face, the excitement of the night's events having not worn off yet.

Jones Jepsen was tried for the murders in Briarwood, where he was ultimately sentenced to death.

On the day of his execution, Jones cackled all the way to the electric chair.

After being strapped to the chair and having a sponge placed upon his greasy scalp to absorb the electricity, Jones was asked if he had any last words.

With this, Jones smiled. He stared into the crowd of onlookers, before settling his eyes on the camera in the center of the room.

His wicked grin growing even larger, Jones said his final words.

"I'll be back."

Also by Devin Cabrera

Welcome to Nightmare Island

Join five friends as they unwittingly embark on a perilous journey to a purportedly state-of-the-art tourist attraction – a haunted island. When they soon discover that they have been lured into a trap, the group must band together to endure the terrifying ordeal of surviving the night while being relentlessly hunted by the most dangerous ghosts the world has ever known. Will they make it out alive, or will they become the next victims of these malevolent spirits? Find out in this gripping page turner that will keep you on the edge of your seat until the very end!

WELCOME TO
NIGHTMARE
ISLAND
DEVIN CABRERA

About the Author

Devin Cabrera developed a passion for stories at a young age, devouring books at every turn. As an adult, this love of stories turned into a career, working on both the big and small screen, bringing characters to life and captivating audiences. With a diverse range of projects under his belt, from gripping dramas such as Pretty Little Liars to thrilling reality shows like Deadliest Catch, he has proven himself as an excellent storyteller in all its forms.

But it wasn't until recently that he decided to turn his talents to the page. Sitting down at his desk, he painstakingly crafted a story, honing every word until it was just right. With a fresh perspective and a lifetime of experience with stories, he promises to take readers on a journey they won't soon forget.